SEX, LOVE& VALENTINES

A collection of twenty erotic stories

Edited by Miranda Forbes

Published by Accent Press Ltd – 2010
ISBN 9781907016103

Copyright © Accent Press Ltd 2010

Printed and bound in the UK

Cover design by
Red Dot Design

Contents

The Heart-Shaped Box
by Justine Elyot

I tend to ignore the advance of Valentine's Day: the steady pink-and-fluffying of the shop windows and card racks; the helium balloons and expensive chocolates and bottles of fizz everywhere; the perfume promotions and special restaurant menus and adverts for *The Twenty Most Vomit-Inducing Ballads in the World, Ever, Part 38*. It all leaves me a bit cold, this commercialisation of love. Not even love. Romance. Whatever *that* is.

So when Spiro told me he had a Valentine's surprise for me, I was unenthusiastic. 'I don't do Valentine's Day,' I told him.

'You will do this one,' he told me, undaunted. 'You will do. And you will be done to.'

Ah, now that sounded more like something I could get on board with. And I began to feel optimistic. Spiro understood me. He would not be like the last boyfriend I had over a Valentine's Day, who gave me a fuchsia-coloured teddy bear wearing a T-shirt bearing the legend "I Wuv U". That was doomed right from the start. The power of wuv was definitely not enough.

With Spiro though, at the age of twenty-eight, I had finally started to explore aspects of my sexual identity that had long lain dormant. I had always known I had a kinky side, but I assumed it was something I ought to hide or suppress, for fear of … I don't really know. But fear kept it in the background, at any rate, while I played at being vanilla and wondered why I couldn't get properly involved in my relationships.

The lovers thought I was cold and self-absorbed, and I probably was. Until Spiro came along.

It was like a lightning flash; he did everything right, the way I fantasised. He watched me for a while first – all the eyes-meeting-and-snatching-away stuff that makes the pit of your stomach bubble and boil fit to burst. Then there were knowing looks and smirks and somehow always being in the elevator at the same time, brushing up, nudging shoulders. Then he deviated from the vanilla script and walked straight into my dreams by following me to the tube station one evening after work and saying, 'You should come out with me. I think I'd be good for you.'

Like any self-respecting noughties woman, I played up the independent schtick and scorned his advance. 'Yeah? Good for me? Right.'

'Because I've seen the type you go for, and I think I know where you're going wrong.'

'Oh, pray do tell.' Heavy on the sarcasm, but my heart was pitter-pattering like a captive bird's.

'You go for these sensitive guys you can walk all over. They don't challenge you, so you get bored and move on. You need someone that challenges you. I'd challenge you.'

The crowds at the ticket barrier blurred away for a moment – I actually felt faint. I mean, it was hardly a revelation – at some level I'd always known this. But … for somebody *else* to see it … it felt significant. And momentous. And a bit like falling in love, not that I'd ever done that.

I went out with him, and he was right. He challenged

me. He interested me. He kept me on my toes. It was weird, because he was two years younger than me, and I'd always fantasised about an older man, but he had a natural authority that went beyond youthful cockiness and self-assurance – though he had those in spades too. It didn't hurt that he was gorgeous either, in that broad-shouldered olive-skinned Italian way, with a shock of inky hair and sumptuous lips you could kiss all day and night.

The sex got very exciting very quickly. There was none of that pussy-foot dance, shall-we-or-shan't-we, 'oh look, I've missed all the buses and I can't afford a taxi' type thing. No, I cooked him a meal and after we'd spooned up the last of the tiramisu, he pushed my wine glass aside and said, 'If we're out of food, it must be time for bed.' A grin that could be interpreted as cheeky or wicked accompanied the words. 'I think you must agree.'

'You're awful,' I said.

'That's for you to find out. Though I don't think you'll be saying so tomorrow morning.'

He wasn't awful. He was amazing. He did all the things I'd longed for other lovers to do – he held me down by the wrists, he talked dirty, he encouraged me to change position by slapping me on the bum, and, most of all, he made me come like the Japanese bullet train, hard and fast and over and over again. He was like a rough, bluff pirate king of sex and I couldn't get enough of him.

So it was just as well he had plenty to give. He was still giving, six months later, in mid-February, just as the celebration of St Valentine hit the cash registers of the post-Christian world.

'You know,' I said to Spiro during coffee break while we watched various colleagues sighing and squealing over bouquets and whatnot, 'it isn't even clear that there *was* a St Valentine. And if there was, he was just some

3

priest that got executed by the Romans. Not a great lover or anything. I don't get how all this has built up around him. I bet he'd be embarrassed.'

'You're so anti-romantic,' said Spiro, linking his ankle with mine and wrenching it back under the chair, one of those little signs of affection that are his signature. 'I think that's why I love you. Anyway, wait till you get home. There's a big surprise for my kinky little kitten.'

'Don't call me a kitten. And I hate surprises.'

'I know. Did anyone ever tell you I'm a sadist?'

We laughed long and low, then kissed, to the amused indulgence of our workmates, who have built up an entire false mythology around our relationship and expect to be asked to crack open the posh hatboxes before summer comes.

At least I'm *expecting* a surprise, I mused to myself on the tube home. I was alone, Spiro having some mysterious business in the West End, all of which was presumably a cover for some nefarious plan or other. All the same I was tense and strung tight with anticipation all the way back along the Metropolitan Line and then all the way along the scruffy road of once-imposing houses where I live in my poorly-converted first-floor flat.

The February chill penetrated my bones, so the first thing I did once I'd hung up my coat and scarf was crank up the heating. I looked warily around me while I punched buttons, half-expecting some ninja assassin to jump out of the wall, but all was quiet, save for the creaky pipes.

The living room yielded no clue as to the nature of my surprise, so I walked on through the bedroom. Aha. There on the bed, a huge red heart-shaped box, almost the width of the duvet, and about half the length. Beneath the ribbon that crossed its surface was a note, which I plucked out and read.

"Dearest Horny Hayley

Inside this box are treats for you and for me. Those for you are wrapped up in tissue paper – those for me are in boxes. You MUST NOT LOOK at the things inside boxes – I will unwrap them and show them to you when I get back. But you are very welcome to open your own presents – I expect you to be wearing/playing with them by the time I arrive, which should be in about one hour. Don't let yourself come before I do though, and, most of all ...

DON'T OPEN THE BOXES!

Always your

Spiro."

Things to wear and things to play with ... I suspected he didn't mean a necklace and a game of Scrabble. Greedily, I whipped off the lid and cast my eye over pale tissue and intriguing boxes of leather and satin-covered card.

The first thing I reached for was soft and squashy – one of the somethings to wear, I surmised, and I found I was right when it turned out to be unexpectedly heavy, falling on to the bed in a liquid pool of blackness. What was it? So shiny and sheeny – oh! Latex underwear! We had discussed this once, in a pre-sex conversation about how we would like to see each other dressed, but it had remained in the realms of fantasy, until now.

Eagerly, I undressed out of my work clothes and struggled into the new acquisitions. It really was a struggle – they were tighter than elastic bands; I had to dust my skin with talcum powder before the shorts would go anywhere near my thighs. And there was something else about them that was special. The bra had little cutaway heart-shapes where the nipples should go, giving

5

a peek-a-boo effect. The cut outs were trimmed with marabou, drawing the eye straight to my chill-hardened nubs. The short shorts were even more scandalous. Crotchless, they sheared away from my bottom, exposing most of it in a similar heart-shaped fur-trimmed frame. They were no more than a plasticised sign shrieking 'LOOK! RUDE BITS HERE!' I looked utterly and ravishingly whorish. I loved them.

What else? A small package revealed a pair of pale-pink rubber hearts, nubbed on the inside. I wasn't sure what they were for, until a glance at the instructions informed me that they were Breast Stimulators. Batteries, I was relieved to see, were included. Frowning a little, unsure of how they worked, I popped one on to a nipple. The soft jelly moulded itself to my skin, the nubs feeling deliciously bumpy. I pressed the button on the control unit and it began a soft vibration, clinging and clamping and massaging so that jolts of pleasure-pain travelled diagonally down to my centre. I cupped the breast with my hand, encouraging further friction and watching myself in the mirror. If one felt good, I reasoned, two had to be even better, so I applied the second and spent a pleasant five minutes letting them do the thing they did best – stimulate me.

They were so effective that I had to switch them off before Spiro's instruction not to come before he did became impossible to obey. What was next? A long, slender item captured my attention, next to a shorter, fatter one. They went together, I sensed. The shorter, fatter one proved to be a bottle of rose-scented lubricant. Which gave me a clue about the other … ah. Anal beads in the shape of tiny red rubbery hearts, threaded together on a flexible string that ended with a heart-shaped flange. I had to snort. Some people's idea of romance … Well, it was pretty much the same as mine. Did Spiro expect me to insert these on my own? We had played with plugs and beads before, but he had always put them inside me while I bent submissively, parting my cheeks for him while he clicked and clucked sounds of encouragement, amid stern injunctions against trying to stop him.

Nothing ventured, nothing gained, and six months with Spiro had fired my adventurous spirit, so I unscrewed the cap of the lube and poured some into an oil burner on the mantel. I coated the beads until they smelled like a flower garden in June, then reached around behind me, prodding at my bum cheeks until I was able to locate the right spot. It was too difficult standing, though, so I spread my feet and bent as far as I could without losing my footing, trying once more to spear my back passage with the soft but unyielding tip of the beads. It was not uncomfortably large, and it edged in without too much trouble, slipping past the gate of my sphincter and advancing along the dark and private recesses of my behind, pulling its companions along in its wake. It took a little while, and I almost cricked my neck reaching around, but eventually all five beads were snugly ensconced and the heart-shaped flange peeked bawdily out between my rounded and welcoming cheeks.

There was no chance of forgetting they were in there, so I had to walk a little delicately back over to the bed to investigate further.

Nothing was left except two interesting boxes – one long and narrow, one small and square. I was half-disappointed that there was no vibrator for me, but also relieved, because that would have been certain death to my promise not to come before Spiro was home. I already felt friskier than a barrel of ferrets and the temptation to put my hand between my thighs and bring myself to the inevitable conclusion those nipple stimulators and anal beads were leading me towards was very strong. I shut my eyes, trying to focus for a second, but then all I could think of was what might be in the boxes. Perhaps the long one *was* a vibrator. The boxes were not ribboned or taped shut in any way – it would be the work of easy seconds to lift the lids and peek …

I bent over the square box and, with the lightest of fingertips, tried to ease it sweetly upwards, thinking for some reason that I would be less likely to be detected if I pretended to be Raffles on the heist of his lifetime. In retrospect, I know that it would have made no difference at all if I had wrenched the thing open and flung its contents to the corners of the room. Because I was being watched.

'Aha!' Spiro kicked open the slightly-ajar door with a flourish, beaming evilly all over his handsome face. 'I *knew* it! I knew you would try to sneak a peek.'

I wheeled around, pouting, feeling a little absurd in my latex whorewear and rubber nipple hearts, not to mention the anal beads jiggling snugly in my behind.

'You mean you laid a trap!'

'Of course I did! Would you expect any less of me?'

He swooped up behind me, patting the bare part of my bottom, making the beads move exquisitely. 'I'm so pleased you fell into it. It means I get to use this.'

He picked up the long, thin box and lifted the lid, slowly and dramatically, holding it under my nose. I gasped and then giggled as the contents were revealed – a slender, flexible rod, topped with a pink heart-shaped piece of leather.

'Oh, you swine! You set me up!'

'I did – and you can't deny that the punishment fits the crime, can you?' He swatted me gently on the behind and then lowered me over the bed with a firm hand to my shoulder until I was bent, hands on the duvet, bottom sticking out in invitation.

'But before we address your misbehaviour,' he said, taking the final box and rattling its contents intriguingly, 'we have one more element to put in place.'

I did not see him open this one, but I soon felt him, probing around my spread pussy lips, pressing something against my clit and then sealing it there with a length of what might have been bondage tape, laid from thigh top to thigh top. I must have looked interesting, all shiny and black where I was not nude, but with my rudest parts exposed and on display, ready to accept the kiss of the crop.

'Are your nipple massagers working?' he asked lightly.

'Yes,' I told him, feeling the bumps against my rock-hard buds, reminded of how very much I would like to come.

'And how do those beads feel, all the way up your arse, dear Valentine?'

He put a hand against the heart-shaped base of the bead rod and gave it a little pull and push, making me wriggle and squeal.

'Oh God! Ohhhh.'

'Just the final touch now,' he promised, and he must have flicked a switch somewhere, because I came into glowing life – whatever was taped against my clit began to buzz, sending waves of merciless sensation to the swollen, oversensitised nexus of nerve endings. I thought I might come there and then, but I was soon distracted by the sharp smack of the crop on my bottom.

I did not know whether to yelp or sigh or beg for more. The crop stung, but in a way that augmented the sensual pleasure of the other instruments that played on my body. The strokes were hard enough to force the anal beads ever deeper and would have dislodged the clit buzzer if it hadn't been strapped to my undercarriage, but they made the pleasurable effects of the nipple massagers more intense, and almost agonisingly erotic. Stroke after stroke fell; I could not have counted them under pain of … more pain … so distracted and discombobulated was I by the entire smorgasbord of sensation. I think I was still breathing, but you'd have had to check because I wouldn't have been able to testify. I pushed my bum out for more, loving every zinging swingeing swipe, loving the way it rattled my beads inside me and kept the pressure on my clit just about bearable with its contrapuntal sharpness; I could have let him spank me all night long.

My orgasm put an end to the punishment, though, ripping through me even as Spiro laid on harder and harder strokes until its tide came out and the red-purpleness in front of my eyes receded. I fell forward on the bed, gibbering something like 'Thank you, Sir,' over and over again, finally understanding the phrase *mindblowing orgasm*. It felt as if my bulbs had been snuffed, my circuitry overloaded and exploded.

My Valentine feast was not over yet though, for even as I lay, face flat on the bed, regaining my wits, Spiro began to fuck me with the handle of the crop, pushing it lazily in and out, keeping the clit buzzer on until I came again, at which point he slowly pulled the beads from my bum, making me wonder if it was possible to die of climaxing, and making me also not care either way.

'So you don't do Valentine's Day, eh?' he asked archly, once I had wobbled to my feet and been taken over to the mirror to inspect my arse, which had a tasteful print of red heart shapes all over it now.

'I may have changed my mind,' I said thickly, having to cling on to him to stay upright.

'Good, good,' he approved, running hands along the curve of my bum, pressing thumbs into some of the scorched hearts. 'So what did you get me?'

'Your favourite,' I said. 'My warm wet mouth.'

As I sank to my knees and unbuttoned his trousers, I reflected that St Valentine probably wouldn't approve of this either.

'I'll love you for ever if you swallow,' hinted Spiro.

Ah, who said romance was dead?

Exposure
by Kat Black

February 13

"11pm tonight," reads the bold scrawl inked across the rectangle of card I pull from the matching scarlet envelope. "Be home and alone. Sit facing the balcony door with a single candle lit close by. Wait. Watch."

My heart seems to stop then starts pounding again high in my throat. The commanding message ends without a signature. The card – luxuriously thick – is devoid of identifying marks. The hand-delivered envelope provides no hint as to the sender.

And I need no clues to tell me who is responsible for sliding the mystery note under my apartment door.

I clench the card, creasing it, as something hot and exciting ignites inside me, stealing all my breath. Already heavily wrapped against the wintry chill of my daily commute, I'm swamped by the sudden, sultry heat held trapped beneath the tailored layers of my clothing. The skin of my neck prickles against my scarf.

Drawn by an irresistible pull, I turn to look across the neat expanse of my living room to the sliding glass door that leads on to my tiny fifth-floor balcony. Not far beyond the frost-encrusted railings, a sleek residential tower identical to the one I'm standing in looms through the murky grey light of dawn.

A random scatter of glowing, golden squares adorns

the tall façade, indicating that other early risers are up and setting about their day. But I only have eyes for the set of windows directly opposite mine. Ones shrouded in darkness, with curtains drawn tight.

Pulse hammering, I stare and wonder if he is there, staring back through a crack in the fabric. Watching me.

He loves to watch, I'd discovered, soon after moving in. But then, so do I, he'd learnt, at around the same time. Ever since that first electric moment of shared awareness, we've been engaged in a game of visual foreplay; tantalising each other and tormenting ourselves with the ultimate *look-but-don't-touch* tease.

Over the months, we've grown ever more confident and daring – wearing less, showing more, thrilling to the danger of getting caught out and adding a whole new dimension to the term "Neighbourhood Watch". And always, we've kept our distance, remained the most perfect of intimate strangers.

Until now.

The card I clasp so tightly in my trembling fingers conveys a message far beyond the written words. It represents a turning point, a promise of something new, something more.

I want to stop and consider the significance of it all, want to muse on all the possibilities and wonder what surprises "11pm tonight" holds. But right now I can't afford to spare the time. Any further delay in departure will make me late for a business meeting that's far too important to miss.

Still staring across at the blank, lifeless windows, I make a show of tucking the card into my overcoat pocket with deliberate movements. Then, with a swivel of my leather-booted heel, I turn back to the door, pausing only to flick off the overhead lights and plunge the room into near-darkness as I leave.

At 10.59 p.m., I allow myself to light the fat church candle sitting ready on my coffee table. The barely contained excitement fizzing through me makes my movements clumsy and I fumble the simple task.

Despite the hectic pace of my day, there's been only one thing playing on my mind. Counting down the past fifteen hours to this final minute, with each and every second passing in a protracted crawl that sparks through every nerve.

Keeping a tight rein on my impatience, I force myself to slow down and concentrate on my preparations.

Candle wick finally aflame, I move around the room, turning off all the lamps and readjusting – yet again – the exact position of the chair I'd earlier dragged away from the dining table. The stereo stays as it is, filling the deeply shadowed background with a slinky mix of *Parisian Lounge* sophistication.

Everything is in place as the stereo's illuminated clock ticks over and displays the magic number at last. Drawing a deep, shaky breath, I head to one side of the balcony door and pull on the cord that opens my vertical blinds.

The orange-tinged darkness of the city night outside is almost a perfect match for the candlelit interior of my apartment, so no reflection mars the expanse of glass in front of me as I sit.

Outside, the air is cold and clear, providing a crisply defined view of the building opposite. Here and there, slivers of light frame windows curtained against the seeping chill.

His windows remain dark but as I peer harder I can just make out a mellow flicker of light around the edges of his balcony door. In a nervous gesture, my hands smooth the silk of my short tunic-dress over the top of my stockinged thighs.

With a suddenness that makes me start, one side of the curtains opposite flicks back, releasing a blaze of golden candlelight. A shadow moves across the glass and then the other curtain is drawn away to reveal ...

Oh my God. A woman.

A naked woman. Sitting in a straight-backed chair and facing out into the night in a position that pretty much mirrors mine. I stare at her in breathless shock, but she doesn't react at all as her eyes are covered by a glossy, blood-red blindfold.

The vivid slash of colour looks startling against the woman's pale skin and fair hair that so resemble my own. And that's when it hits me. Is she supposed to *be* me?

The heels of my palms press into my thighs. Whatever I'd been expecting from him tonight, it wasn't anything close to this.

My eyes flick to him as he steps behind the woman's chair. Tall and strong and bare from the hips up, he appears more beautiful than ever with the glow from numerous candles gilding his lean torso. He looks directly ahead and although we're too distant for me to clearly see his eyes, I know he is zeroing in on my single candle flame, using it as a reference point to find me in the shadows.

He waits for a moment, keeping that watchful attention focused my way, then places his hands on the woman's shoulders and runs them in a slow and sensuous slide up the curve of her neck until his fingers bracket either side of her jaw. He pauses there, keeping the woman in a hold that looks both possessive and dominating as he smiles wickedly across the night-time void that separates us.

The world seems to tilt and I can hardly breathe as I begin to fully realise his voyeuristic intent. He's going to use the woman to show me the things he wants to do to me, to demonstrate the way it would be between us. He wants me to watch as he touches me, makes love to me through her.

I couldn't look away if I wanted to.

He forces the woman's chin up as he bends his dark head to speak in her ear. A moment later she smiles and raises a hand in a little wave. The woman's smile drops into an open-mouthed gasp as he tilts her head to one side and runs his tongue over her cheek. Turning her face upwards, he covers her mouth with his and from the working of his jaw and the motion of his head, I can see it's a deep and passionate claiming right from the start.

My fingers curl around the hem of my dress as I watch, ensnared, imagining it's me sitting in that other chair, tasting the wet heat of his kiss. My lips part and my tongue slips out to run along the seam, instinctively searching out his essence.

Opposite, the woman raises her arms to wrap about his neck but he pulls away and captures her hands. I can see the lowered brows, the stern expression she's blind to. Can see his lips move as he speaks to her again while locking her hands together behind her neck.

Still standing behind her, he brings his own hands around either side of her body and cups her breasts in his palms, his olive-toned skin a stark contrast to the woman's alabaster paleness. I bite my lip as I watch his fingers and thumbs close around the delicate pink of her nipples.

My own breasts tingle, nipples springing to full erectness. I fancy I can feel the warmth of those large

16

palms covering my naked skin, feel the strength of those fingers squeezing and pinching until the first delicious sting of pain. My breath hitches.

As though my desires are somehow transmitted across the night, the woman arches suddenly under his hands, her mouth opens on a cry. I hear a gasp and realise my own body is bowed in sympathy.

Under a barrage of plucks and twists, she squirms, but doesn't try to lower her arms as he keeps a steady stream of words pouring over her. I'd give anything to be able to hear what it is he's saying; to know whether it's the power of the words themselves or the timbre of his voice that binds her so obviously to his will.

My own stomach muscles flutter and clench when his hands skim down over her ribs and belly. He bends over her, going lower still, covering her upper thighs with his palms. Pulling her legs apart, he spreads her wide.

I shift a little to look past an inconveniently positioned railing bar and even that small movement causes arrowheads of fire to shoot from the hot, tingly place between my legs. Moaning, I press my own legs together and rock my pelvis, rubbing myself against the seat of the chair. I can't quite tell from here how ready the other woman is, but from the sticky feel of my knickers, I'd bet she's no wetter than I am.

Without letting up on the fast, demanding pace he's set from the start, he plunges one hand straight between her legs. The other rises again to her breasts, sharing attention between them. His muscles shift and flex and the woman writhes as he invades her most vulnerable flesh with the kind of commanding mastery I've only ever dreamt about.

The banging of my heartbeat grows louder; drowns out the smooth strains of the music as I watch him drive her ruthlessly, relentlessly towards a place of pure surrender. There is nothing gentle in his stance or his movements, but riding his touch hard, the woman obviously loves every second of what he's doing.

As do I.

My thighs fall open, making room for my fingers to stroke their way up the insides. Carried on the rising heat of my body, the needy scent of my own musk floats up to fill my nostrils. My skin feels drawn too tight – so sensitive that even the cool brush of silk has me shuddering with every move.

My fingers find the barrier of my knickers, rub over the damp warmth seeping through the crotch. A deep, heavy pressure sits low in my belly, pushing down behind my clitoris until I can feel the beat of my pulse throbbing there. I press the pad of my middle finger down over the spot and gasp.

On the candlelit stage opposite, he withdraws his hand from between the woman's legs and straightens slightly. Raising the hand to his mouth, he makes me watch as he takes his time to lick and suck his fingers clean before bending again to sink them into her waiting depths.

Unable to bear any more waiting of my own, I burrow my fingers under the edges of my knickers. It's sultry under there. My labia feel flushed and swollen. Heat and moisture trace the seam of my slit. I part myself and explore my hot, hidden folds. I'm ripe and juicy as a summer fruit, instantly coating my fingers with slick juices.

The fact that he has me so primed in so short a time without even touching me is staggering. I've no idea how, but by some amazing providence he seems to understand my most intimate desires and fantasies. He's the nearest to a perfect lover I've ever found.

I moan and spread my legs wider, beginning to mimic what I see happening through the glass. In less than a minute I'm on the verge of orgasm.

The woman starts to thrash and buck. His hand rises from her breasts to her mouth, fingers pushing past her lips to anchor themselves deep inside, restraining her. And just like that he sets us both off.

She melts against his strength as he draws out her climax with his fingers and his words. I feel a spike of jealousy before I realise his attention is focused outwards, towards me. I shake and shudder and pant, wringing every last drop of pleasure from myself for him, giving him everything even though he can't see it.

Boneless, I slump in the chair. The fine sheen of perspiration dampening my skin is given no chance to cool as he steps around the woman, hands busy on the front of his jeans. I burn with renewed heat as they drop away to reveal his cock, standing thick and hard and flushed against his belly.

Stepping clear of the denim, he guides the woman off the chair and takes her place, positioning his long legs to either side as she goes down onto her knees in front of him.

He wraps his hands in her hair and pulls her head towards his groin. The angle doesn't allow me to see the moment that his erection disappears into her mouth, but I know precisely when it happens from the tightening of his features.

I wonder how big he feels to her; how warm and solid and satiny as he glides over her tongue? And his taste ... is it sharp and salty with pre-come already or all earthy male?

I swallow as my mouth waters.

He wastes no time in urging the woman into a strenuous, uncompromising rhythm. He continues to talk to her all the while, although I notice the words come in ever shorter bursts; sometimes getting caught behind tightly pursed lips, sometimes being forced out between gritted teeth.

The woman's hands, now free of their invisible bonds, disappear between his legs. His chest heaves and his arms pump in time with her bobbing head. More and more frequently his head dips to watch her work him with mouth and hands.

I want to watch too. So badly, my nose is pressed right up against the door before I'm aware of having left my seat. The heat of my breath clouds the cold glass in front of my face and I jump back, not wanting to miss a moment.

The pressure and the ache are back in my pelvis. I widen my stance, planting my stilettos a shoulder-width apart, and cup myself through my clothing. Rolling my hips, I grind myself into my palm, imagining how the steel-hard length of him looks slipping wetly between the woman's lips.

I groan, tortured. Needing more.

I want him to fuck her. Right now. Want him to bend her over the back of that chair and take her from behind while he looks at me and comes apart hard.

I will it across the night but it does no good. He keeps the woman on her knees, working her harder and faster until his entire body draws taut.

Eyes closed, he throws his head back. Even from here I can see the definition of straining tendons as he remains locked like that for one two heartbeats.

Then he lowers his head and opens his eyes to look directly into my apartment.

Using his grip on the woman's hair, he drives her face all the way into his crotch, meeting her there with a final, spearing thrust. His tightly braced muscles twitch and his lips pull back on the roar of his release. I feel the shockwaves of it reverberating right down to my core, even though it's an utterly silent sound to me. In that moment I come again, crying out loud enough for both of us.

February 14

I stumble to avoid stepping on the envelope that flops at my feet when I open my front door the following morning. It's larger and thicker than the one delivered yesterday but I can see instantly that the vivid scarlet colour is exactly the same.

My pulse, which has been revving all morning at the memories of last night, accelerates flat out as I bend to retrieve the envelope, then nearly stalls completely as I tear open the flap to reveal a red satin blindfold folded inside.

Another thick piece of card nestles alongside it. I pull it free and as my vision blurs I can barely read the words:

"11pm tonight. Be mine."

Beer Bottle
by Jeremy Edwards

It was 2 a.m., and I was cleaning up after the Valentine's Day party. I couldn't actually remember how or why it had become an annual tradition for me to throw a big party on an occasion more conventionally celebrated by breaking up into small groups of two or three. But in my circle, people seemed to like it, even the couples.

Beer bottles dotted the landscape of my living room. I plucked each one from its niche and ferried them all into the kitchen. Some of them still had beer in them – as much as half a bottle, in some cases. I emptied them into the sink.

Except one. It was on the right-hand stereo speaker, and I knew it was Eveline's. I could still see her sitting on the floor and putting it up there, skilfully, without looking. The small label around the neck of the bottle had a tiny, precise tear in it, and I remembered seeing her tear it while she spoke to my upstairs' neighbour.

After all the other bottles had been cleared away, I picked up Eveline's and examined it. Why, I wondered, would someone drink all but a half-centimetre's worth of a bottle of beer? I thought about it, and reasoned that someone might do this as a way of resisting the temptation of a second beer, if her judgment told her she shouldn't. If you haven't, technically, finished Beer the First, then you won't pick up Beer the Second, right?

I didn't know if that had been Eveline's motivation. But regardless of the reason for its condition, this not-quite-empty bottle symbolized one thing to me – unfinished business. To my mind, it was inextricably related to the opening she'd left me when she had departed: "I'll be up for a while, if you want to call me." Though she had not been the last to leave, the few remaining partyers had soon said their goodnights. Even after my perfunctory clean-up, I judged that only about fifteen minutes had elapsed since I'd hugged her goodbye.

I swigged the barely significant remnants of Eveline's beer. In reality, it tasted only like flat beer, but I fantasized that it tasted like her. I closed my eyes and imagined smelling it on her breath, as she leaned in close for a kiss. I contemplated how the beer would taste on her tongue … and then I contemplated how her tongue would feel on my cock. I wanted another sip from this bottle – but it was bone-dry now.

I hesitated only a moment before heading for the phone, still holding the ghost of her drink. Hey, I assured myself, she'd said to call if I felt like it… and I felt like it.

It took her a good five rings to answer. "Sorry, Jim," she explained. "I just got home, and I had to take a wicked piss." Pissing away the beer she drank at my place, I thought. Why did she need to go home to do that? She could have peed right here. Maybe she would even have let me watch. Anyway, whether Eveline would have been an open- or closed-door pisser tonight, I was wishing she hadn't left.

I gave voice to that last emotion. "It's too bad you went home," I said. "It's rather pleasant here now, with the place quiet. We could have talked."

She laughed. "We *are* talking."

"Good point," I acknowledged. "But … look, why

don't you come back?"

"Huh? Now?"

"Why not? We're both night owls. You know neither of us is ready to go to sleep. We could just pretend you never left. We could – y'know – hang out."

"I guess, but …"

"It's a beautiful night, you're only fifteen minutes away, and …" My smooth come-on softened into something more sensitive. "And I'd really like it if you came over, now that I can give you my full attention."

Her voice also became a little quieter, a little more delicate. "You're talking me into it."

"If you don't, we'll just end up yakking for two hours on the phone anyway. Why not do it face to face?" That's what I wanted. To do it face to face with Eveline.

"OK," she said. "Yeah. Actually, that would be nice. Very nice. I'll see you soon." And she hung up.

Another fifteen minutes elapsed, during which I intended to do a little more cleaning up. Instead, I found myself sitting at the kitchen table, thinking about Eveline. My mind raced around from calculating when we'd first met to daydreaming about how good she looked when she was naked to wondering how her dissertation was coming along. When the doorbell rang, I was a little surprised that the erection that had developed during the how-good-she-looked-naked portion of the stream of consciousness had survived the dissertation portion quite well.

"Thanks, Jim. I'm glad I came back," she volunteered as soon as I'd closed the door behind her. "Subconsciously, I think I was hoping all along that the night wasn't over." She looked me in the eye. "Did you notice I didn't finish my beer?"

"Of course."

"Did you finish it for me?"

"Of course."

She removed her coat and flopped unceremoniously onto my couch – on her belly, with her feet on the armrest. Eveline and I had long ago stopped standing on ceremony, and I loved that.

She turned her head toward me, sociably, as I made myself comfortable on the floor beside her.

"So … " I said.

"Yeah," she concurred.

We both knew that this elliptical conversation was about "us". Eveline and I had never been able to make up our minds as to whether we wanted to be lovers or just friends, and all roads led to that question.

We left the question lying there for a few minutes while we just enjoyed each other's quiet company, both of us zoning out in the pocket of our long-established bond.

"Handle my ass a while, would you?" she said after a bit. "It helps me think."

No, we didn't stand on ceremony, Eveline and I.

I massaged the seat of her jeans, stroking and fondling her soft cheeks. "Do you really think that my caressing your marvellous behind is going to help you think objectively about our relationship?"

Her smile was a broad one. "Who said I wanted to think *objectively*?"

And so, inevitably, the jeans bowed out of the picture, as they had so many times before. Tonight the cotton bikini panties were pale blue with multicoloured stripes. Eveline's ass looked like that fruit-striped cartoon zebra from the chewing-gum commercials – only significantly rounder and much, much more lovely. I told her all this, and she responded with a very un-zebra-like purr. I squeezed and kneaded her. I listened to her breathing becoming irregular. She was getting very aroused – and

25

so was I.

Then I tickled the erogenous skin just within the elastic, and I watched Eveline's ass wiggle its ass off.

And so, inevitably, the panties bowed out of the picture, too.

Even with her pussy now exposed, it was all about her ass for a bit longer. This is how it had been on previous occasions, and this was just fine with both of us. I couldn't get enough of kissing those friendly cheeks, or of grazing the crack with my nose while I held her adorable legs behind the knees.

Eveline had the most satisfying ass I'd ever handled – the classic Ass Next Door, if you will (though she didn't live quite *that* close to me). I'd known candy-apple asses and ice-cream-scoop asses. Boutique asses and museum-quality asses. Sturdy, bike-riding cheeks and delicate pleasure-globes. Flesh that smelled like vanilla, like berries, like honey. But Eveline's was simply the perfect ass, in my view. What a philosopher would call a *platonic,* or ideal, ass – though my friendship with it, at the moment, was anything but "platonic". It was an ass that would have seemed like a beautiful abstraction, were it not so wonderfully tangible. Its roundness never failed to attract me; its smoothness never failed to seduce me; and its responsiveness never failed to arouse me. It was an ass I could engage with all night.

But I knew how wet she was becoming. I could tell from her intoxicating giggles, and from the delicious feminine aroma that was wafting up. This wetness invited and required my fingers. I inserted a pair and Eveline squeezed them, and her luscious bottom wriggled anew beneath my face.

When it became unthinkable to continue interacting without our genitals being joined, we helped each other

26

undress. She had not worn a bra beneath her sleek turtleneck, and her breasts rushed out to greet me. My own body appeared, thin and persistently boyish as always, when jeans and briefs and polo shirt joined her clothes in the garment orgy on the floor. Our torsos pressed together, my erection sought her sex, and we merged back onto the couch – rather gracefully, I thought, for a couple of confused lover-friends.

We mingled with ease, the vital connection freeing us from emotional ambivalence and from the desperate libidinous tension that had gripped us while we hurried to undress. Now, each moment was paradise: we basked, we wallowed, and we ascended effortlessly into ecstasy. Eveline pulled my upper body tightly against hers with one bare arm, while sensuously raising the other for me. I kissed the inviting cavity it revealed and allowed myself to become engulfed in the delirious fragrance of her flesh. At another latitude, I rhythmically jiggled her warm ass cheeks, as my cock and her cunt squirmed together like the old pals they were.

When I spouted, almost without consciousness of what my prick was doing, her undulating coos slipped over the threshold into shrieks of laughter. Her bottom, still cupped in my hand and warm with the flush of her excitement, tickled my palm with its involuntary tremors, as she quickly rubbed herself to climax against the welcoming bolster of my spent body. The methodical effectiveness of her sweet friction reminded me of the precise way she'd torn the label on that beer bottle.

She spoke first. "So," she sighed. Then she gave a short, happy chuckle.

"Yeah," I agreed. I kissed her hair.

Maybe the fact that we had this communication thing down meant that we were right for each other, after all.

27

Continuity
by Shanna Germain

The dress is gorgeous; the saleswoman suggested a size smaller than I'd planned and it went on perfectly, skimming the curves of my ass and hips just right, making me look like I have more boobs than I actually do. Fantastic fit, fantastic dress. Billy was going to love it.

Except that now I can't get it off. It's stuck somewhere between my breasts and my shoulders, and my hands and head are caught inside what seems to be an ever-tightening vice-grip of material. Where is Billy and his sexy-sharp knife when you need him?

In some alternate universe, this would be sexy. The saleswoman would be a smart, voluptuous thing who would use my pseudo-bondage to her advantage, the dressing room would be bigger than a postage stamp and I would be able to breathe right now. Instead, I'm starting to wonder if it isn't time to give up this yearly fuckfest with Billy, since it seems to be more work than pleasure at the moment.

But as soon as I think it, I realize that it's a stupid idea – Billy and I have spent every Valentine's day together since our divorce eight years ago, no matter what's going on in our lives, and I know it's something that we both look forward to. I don't want to live with the man again, not ever, but do I want to fuck him hard once a year and see those chocolate-brown eyes of his widen when he looks at me in a dress like this? Oh yes.

My phone goes off again, a jaunty jingle that sounds, oddly enough, like dial phones used to. It's a sound I haven't heard in nearly a year, and it means Billy's calling. He programmed the sound last year when I saw him, saying that he didn't want his name to be associated with either of the other options, which he called Bach-in-elevator and rap-in-rave-party. "Besides," he said, "This is old, like us. So it's perfect." I would have swatted him, but my wrists were still bound with his belt – he liked to tie me up and tease me with one hand, brushing his fingertips over the inside of my thighs, while he did normal things, like twiddle around with my phone.

We always did fuck so well. It was the other things that kept screwing us up. So we made this promise: get together every Valentine's night. Fuck our brains out. Go back to our lives. No more, no less. It was a win-win-win: it kept us tied together in way that seemed important for both of us, it meant we got one great fuck a year no matter who else we were or weren't dating, and it gave us a chance to vet our current partners – if they weren't okay with the Valentine's arrangement, then they weren't right for us. I've let go of at least two potential lovers because they had a shit fit over the deal, and I know Billy's lost more than a few women who had meltdowns at the very idea. I don't think either of us regrets it though. Or at least, I hope not. I've thought, at times, about calling Billy up, seeing if he would want more than a once-a-year bang, but I don't. I know it would ruin everything.

"Your phone is ringing," the saleswoman says helpfully.

"Thank you," I mumble. My voice has that grumpy edge to it that I don't like, but that I've come to accept over the years as being part of me.

"Shall I get my manager?" she asks. I try to remember what her name is – Kathy? Karen? – she told me, but this isn't the kind of place where people wear nametags and I couldn't see it even if she did.

"Out," I say. This is the simplest, most direct command I can think of, and it actually comes out sounding like a real word. "Get me out of this dress."

"How?" she asks. She's given up on the tugging, and I have this image of her standing there, her arms crossed over her chest, staring at me.

"However you can. I don't care."

I call Billy back without listening to his message. I'm driving back to work, Blue Tooth headset blinking in my ear, one hand on the wheel, the other fingering the smooth vinyl curves of the dress. I bought it after all, a size larger than the one I tried on. It won't curve around my hips quite as well, but I don't think I'll get stuck inside it either. Nor will I have another pair of red marks on my neck and shoulders from where a confused and timid saleswoman joined forces with a rather meaty black man to yank a too-tight dress off my head with a dual tug that nearly took my ears off.

Billy's phone clicks on, and I chime in before he can even speak. This is the advantage of knowing each other for nearly twenty years; you don't have to waste time on preliminaries. "Billy, you have to hear what happened to me this afternoon."

"Zoe," he says, and as always, the sound of my name coming from his lips always makes me a little breathless. He has these great lips, big and soft, that contrast with the sharp angles of his cheekbones and his jaw, and the way he brushes them over my breasts, my nipples, saying my name the whole time, over and over, it causes a reaction

30

that's hard-wired into my body, I swear.

I laugh, and the sound is deep and throaty. "Of course, Zoe," I say. "Unless you have some other ex-wife who's dialling you back to tell you about her pre-Valentine's day fiasco."

Silence. But he's laughing soundlessly, I know it.

"Well, do you want to hear your ex's story? Or shall I tell you in person tomorrow? Speaking of tomorrow …" I'm stupidly, suddenly, all aflutter, bouncing around subjects like a coked-up insect. "What's the plan?" We rotate each year. Last year was mine – I tend to use my house, focus on the food and the outfit and the fucking, while Billy likes to go somewhere new, dump us in some wild and crazy place. One year, he dragged me camping, which I would have hated if I hadn't ended up tied to a tree while he curled his fingers inside me, making me howl into the night like some kind of feral creature. Another year, he rented a laser tag place and we fought and skirmished through the night before we finally fucked, wild with competition and pent-up arousal. So I'm excited to see where we're headed. At this point, I just hope my little red dress isn't going to be too out of place.

"About tomorrow …" he says slowly, so slowly I have time to shift gears and narrowly miss a little red Honda that is creeping over into my lane. "That's why I called. Did you get my message?"

Something pings in the bottom of my stomach, rough and dark. I know that sound in his voice. It's the "I have something to tell you but I don't want to" edge. I suddenly wish I'd waited until tonight to call him. "What? No, I was … busy."

There's silence. Too much silence, and I take the moment to signal and find a place to pull off the road and

31

park. My hands are shaking on the wheel, and I wipe my palms off on my pants. It's not even hot. Granted, it's been a shit day, and I haven't eaten enough and I spent most of my morning mummified in man-made materials, but still. I know this reaction is all about Billy, all about what I'm afraid he's going to say next. I rest my forehead on the dashboard, listening to him breathe through my headset, as though his mouth is actually at my ear.

I start to say something, and he starts to say something at the same time and it ends up nothing more than garble. Cars pass me, whizzing by, their sound the only thing in my ear. I wait, let Billy speak.

"There's a girl."

"And …?" The word comes out sounding okay, sounding off-the-cuff, like it doesn't really matter, like I can't imagine what would really matter about some girl, but it hurts to say it, like it scratched my throat on the way up. Such a simple word. How can it hurt so much? It's like I know what he's going to say, even though he hasn't said it yet. If there's a girl, and he's hesitating, it must be *the* girl. The one who is coming to mean so much to him that he's willing to give me up. To give us up.

I finger the vinyl dress in the bag next to me. Such a great dress. Such a waste. If I focus on the dress, I won't cry. Or if I do, I can blame it on the dress instead of on whatever else is bouncing around in my head. After all, it's not like I love Billy – oh, I mean I love him, but not in that way any more, not the way I did in the early years of our marriage. It's not like I want him back. But I like being connected to him, still tied to those good years we had, to our youth. All of which makes my breath go someplace else, someplace where I can't seem to get it back.

"Well, I really, I really like her, Zoe."

"And?"

"And …" A breath. His. I know it's not mine because I can't breathe yet. "I told her about our agreement."

"And?" Why, oh, why can't I say something, anything else? I close my lips, vow not to say anything until I can come up with something functional and intelligent.

"She wants to come."

My head rests on the steering wheel. There are cars going by, still. I know my breath is going in and out, in and out. But I don't feel or hear any of it.

His voice on the other end goes staticy and then clears up. "She wants to come with us. To, you know –" For as good and direct as Billy is in bed, he sometimes can't find the words. I'm not sure I can either, but then they fall out of my mouth.

"She wants a threesome?"

"She does."

"Jesus, Billy."

"I know."

And then there is another kind of silence. Shared. The kind where two people are on the same mindwave, where first you say that you understand the other person, and then you realize that you really do understand the other person, because for a moment you're one and the same.

"Okay, so is this the kind of, 'I want to check out what I'm up against and the only way to do it is to go along?' Or what?"

"Come on, Zoe. You know me better than that."

I do, of course. He has good taste in women. Smart taste. Psychos don't last very long with Billy. They never have.

"I need to think about this," I say. "I bought a dress and everything. Okay, that was a stupid thing to say,

33

wasn't it?"

"Maybe?" he says. "How good of a dress is it?"

"Red. Vinyl. Short as shit. I can barely get into it."

That small intake of breath on the other end of the line, a sound I've always loved to hear. "Black boots?" he asks.

"The leather ones you bought me." For our fifth anniversary. They're still my favourite boots. Billy's too.

"Mmm …"

"Can I think about it?" I ask.

"Of course you can think about it. She's cute. She's smart. She's bisexual."

"I still need to think about it," I say.

"I know," he says. "Call me tomorrow and let me know?"

"Yes," I say. My real life is sliding back in. The clock on the dash says I'm already late getting back to work. My stomach growls grumpily at me.

"Okay," he says. "And, Zoe?"

"Yeah?"

"Say yes. Please. I really dig this girl."

"Call you tomorrow, Billy."

I hang up and wait for the little daggers to poke at my heart, for their sharp ends to sink into the sensitive skin, but nothing happens. In fact, there's a kind of glee, a hopefulness. I want Billy to be happy, I always have. If this girl can give him that, without taking away from us … Although having her there would change everything, wouldn't it? Of course it would. Good? Bad? I can't even begin to imagine.

Early the next morning, Billy sends me a text.

Red head. Did I say smart? Did I say likes girls? Did I say this won't change anything between us?

34

It's the longest text he's ever sent me. I send him one back. A simple word that answers both the text questions and the one he'd asked yesterday.

Yes.

I'm not saying yes because of the girl. Not really. I've never fucked a girl, never so much as kissed one but I'm not averse to it. I'm interested, actually. But I'm saying yes because I trust Billy. Because one of the reasons we fuck so well is that he pushes me beyond everything I think I want or can handle. Because he knows my boundaries better than I do, and he is expert at nudging me just beyond them. He's the first man I had pleasurable anal sex with, the first man I fucked in a public place, the first man who tied my wrists and ankles to the bed and then spent a whole night teasing and teasing, never once letting me come.

The Stanford, he texts. *Room 1215. Six o'clock.*

I'm surprised that he picked a hotel, and then I realize it's a smart choice. With as much as we're going to have going on, a simple, clean place that's close to home seems like the perfect place.

I don't have to text him back that I'll be there. I know he knows.

I get nervous. I *am* nervous. It's been a long time since I was this wound up about fucking, or getting fucked. Not just with Billy, but with anyone. In some ways, I've missed it. That rush, the ping-ping-ping of my heart against my breastbone, the way my clit echoes and murmurs along with it.

Nervous in vinyl is bad though, and I wipe my palms discreetly – or not so discreetly – on my car's fabric seats before I get out. The dress fits like a dream, especially since I know I can get out of it eventually. My black

35

leather boots click-click across the hotel lobby, a sound that's always turned me on, even if they're on my own feet. I've pinned my hair up, loose and wavy, so that Billy can pull it out and fist his hands into it the way he likes.

As I head toward the elevator, the guy behind the check-in counter gives me one of those almost subtle "I don't want to get fired, but I can't help it" once-overs which, okay, I'm not ashamed to admit, does a whole lot for my confidence right now.

The hotel is busy, being a romantic holiday, which means there are too many people and too many pheromones crammed into too small an elevator. I try to see if one of the girls is Billy's, but there's no redhead. Nothing that fits his type. Which, truly, is usually a lot like me – curvy in the ass, no top to speak of, natural in the makeup.

No one gets off with me on the twelfth floor, and it's just me and my nerves standing in front of room 1215. I stand outside for a moment, imagining them, imagining her riding him, or his nails trailing down the curves of her breasts, making her shiver. I've imagined women fucking Billy before – we've talked about current lovers, past lovers, future lovers. This is wholly different. I wait to see if there's a pang of something like remorse or jealousy. Nothing. Nothing except the way the image of them is making me wet. I haven't worn anything beneath the dress and just standing there, my thighs are damp.

I knock.

The girl who answers the door is just a little shorter than me, but she's barefoot and I've got three-inch heels sunk into the hotel carpet. She's also naked. Skinnier than I would have expected, but with a bit of swell at the hips, a bit at the chest. Her nipples are small and pink, already extended. Long red hair waves around her shoulders and a pair of dark green eyes study me intently as she tilts her head. She's not my age, maybe five years younger, old enough to have a few fine lines around her mouth when she gives me a wide, big-toothed smile.

"Oh, yum," she says. "You're as gorgeous as Billy said. Fantastic dress. Come in, come in." She takes my wrist in her fingers when she says this, and pulls me into the room.

I like her instantly. How can I not?

"Thanks," I say, but it's belated. The room is gorgeous. Simple but comfortable. A little sitting area is split off from the bed by a white paper screen. Nice lighting. Unobtrusive decor. My red dress and her red hair are the brightest things in the room.

"I'm Katy," she says. Her hand is still on my wrist. She seems so reactive, so excitable, that I have an odd temptation to pull her against me, to see how she sounds.

"Zoe," I say.

She smiles again, a bit of heat in her expression. "Oh, I know," she says. "I've heard all about you."

"Oh, great," I say, and I laugh as I say it. She leads me to the couch, and lets go of my wrist. From here I can see into the bedroom, the wide bed, the empty room.

"Where's Billy?" I ask.

"He thought … " She sits on the couch, her legs closed at the knees, cute little feet splayed. "He thought we might want a bit of time, to you, know, say hello. As it were."

"Drink?" She reaches for the iced champagne bottle near the coffee table then sits back without picking it up. Her demeanour changes slightly, and she lowers her gaze to her hands. "I'm kind of nervous, I have to admit. Okay, I'm a lot nervous. Really. Really nervous."

I almost have to laugh – she talks just like I do when

I'm uncomfortable. Jesus, Billy really is in trouble this time. And she really is nervous; she's rubbing her hands together like she might start a fire if she does it long enough. I thought I'd be the one who felt out of place, skulking around like the old flame that I am. But somehow knowing she's come here, for Billy, despite her fear, it makes me feel more secure. It makes me like her more.

I take a second to consider. I could sit on the other couch, watch her nervousness, echo it with my own. Or I could move forward, make this easier on us both.

I choose the latter, even though it's not my norm – I'm the passive one with Billy, always – sliding the coffee table away from where she's sitting. I go down on my knees in front of her carefully, a hand on each of her knees, moving slow so I don't fall down in this tight dress, so I don't startle her or me.

"Then let's get to know each other, shall we?" I watch her eyes while I draw a finger along the inside of her pale thighs. Her eyes are so big I can see the whites around them, but she doesn't flinch or pull away.

I dip my head, drawing my tongue over the path that my finger just traced, tasting her skin. She shivers instantly, a small sound of surprise rising from her mouth.

"I thought …" she starts.

"What?" I say as I touch the closely shorn hair between her thighs, the reddish-brown curls soft beneath my fingertips.

"Well, I just assumed … Billy said you were … submissive."

"Oh, I usually am." My laugh has fallen down into my throat, making the sound low and husked, aroused. And then I lean down and dip my tongue into her curls, splitting them with a sweep of the tip, opening her up so that I can taste her. She's sweet and carameled, like maple syrup candy, and she rises up, pushing into my touch.

"Oh," she says, like she understands. I wonder if she does. No one understands Billy and me. But maybe this one will. Maybe she will be the one for him, the one that lets him have the past while moving into the future.

She rises her hips off the couch, her hands finding my head, fingers weaving loosely in my hair. I brush my tongue between the cleft of her, feel her grow wetter against my touch. She is so responsive, bucking and groaning, the muscles in her thighs pulling tight.

The door opens, a soft click and close that makes something drop through my stomach. I can tell without even looking that it's Billy. The air smells faintly of him, a spiced musk that matches his gravelled voice. "I leave you alone for two minutes and look what happens." But I can hear that he's glad.

At the sound of his voice, I suck from her, wanton and hard, letting the taste of her fill my mouth. She tries to hold back, uncertain, torn between the two of us, but Billy takes two steps across the room and stands behind her, dipping his fingers into her hair, holding her still with his fists around his curls.

"Make her come, Zoe," he says.

I hardly have to do anything. Her clit's already a beating pulse against my mouth at his words, and I flick my tongue across her again and again, the movements growing harder until she's bucking and groaning and calling his name in her heated voice.

"Fuck," she says as she falls back to the couch, breathing hard.

I raise my head, meet Billy's questioning, heated gaze over her head. The arousal in his eyes is obvious and intense, and I have a funny feeling it mirrors my own. He lets his gaze travel down the length of my body where I'm crouched, taking in the curves beneath the red dress. It burns me in the way that makes my body feel molten, alive. This, I think, is why we get together every Valentine's day, why our bodies come together in a way that is ever-changing, ever heated. Can I predict what comes after? No. But I never could. I can only close my eyes and hope.

"Yes," I say to Billy's unanswered question.

It's all he needs to hear. He walks around the couch, pulls me up, and slides his hands beneath the dress, giving a soft groan of appreciation when his fingers find my bare curves.

"You too, Katy," he says. His voice is command built from lust, impossible to resist.

From her spot on the couch, Katy leans forward, the soft press of her lips against my thigh, her fingers following Billy's upward, until I can't tell whose touch is where. All I know is that there are two sets of hands caressing my skin beneath the dress, two sets of lips sliding against my skin, three quiet groans of pleasure beginning to fill the room.

No Stopping
by Landon Dixon

She had her thumb out just past the junction of Highways 395 and 190. I was hauling ass – making good time – barrelling down out of the cool Sierra Nevadas and roaring across the harsh, hot flats below. I shot her a quick glance as I motored by, did a double-take; she was a looker. I pumped the brakes, hesitating, then stomped down on the pedal, slewing over to the shoulder of the shimmering asphalt.

I was hell-bent for LA, things to do and people to see, miles to go before I slept with anyone. I didn't have time to stop and smell the hitchhikers. But, I thought, what the hell? It'd been a long, hard, lonely drive from Chicago and a little innocent conversation wouldn't slow me down any.

I drummed the steering wheel of the rumbling car, watching in the rearview mirror as she ran towards me – twin, reddish-brown ponytails flopping, breasts bouncing free and easy beneath a green tank top, legs flashing brown and smooth in a pair of khaki shorts and black boots. She had a big, Army-style pack strapped to her back, a beaded choker around her neck. And as she pulled even with the rear bumper, I noticed that she wasn't any flighty teen queen thumbing a summer away; she was a woman, a woman in her mid-to-late-forties.

She yanked the door open, shrugged off the backpack

and stowed it in the back seat, slid inside. The dust and dry, oven-hot air of the road came with her. She slammed the door shut and said, "Hi. Thanks."

I stared into the brightest, bluest eyes I'd ever seen. They were shining pools in a sun-browned, pretty face. I pulled away from her eyes, gave the rest of her the once-over, taking in her freckled chest, the warm, inviting depth of her cleavage, the twin points indenting the thin material of her top, her slim, supple arms and legs. There were crow's feet spreading out from the corners of her eyes and laugh lines around her mouth, and her chest hung a little low, but, somehow, all that only enhanced her seasoned good looks. She smelled surprisingly fresh, clean.

"No problem," I said, glancing at my watch. Time was a-wasting. It stopped for no man, or woman. I punched the accelerator, fishtailed back onto the highway in a spray of gravel. "Where're you headed?"

"Anywhere."

I shot her another look. She was staring straight ahead, hands in her lap, smile tugging on the edges of her lips.

The car ate up the road, like there was no stopping it.

The last thing I wanted, or needed right then, was to get mixed up with some mixed-up broad fumbling her way through a mid-life crisis, looking to drag down the first thing in pants that drove by, ride him for the thrills and the food money. But I'd picked her up for conversation, so ten miles down that melting ribbon of black tar, I started some.

"What's your story?" I said.

She told me. Man, did she tell me. But I guess I asked for it.

42

She'd gotten hitched when she was only eighteen – to her high school history teacher sweetheart – and long story short, three kids and twenty-seven years of marriage later, the cradle-robbing educator had died, leaving her the emptiest of nests. So she'd flown the coop, the little house on the Nebraskan prairie, and ventured out into the big, bad world – to see what she could see, experience new and different things.

"A second childhood, huh?" I grunted, reaching over and cranking up the A/C, brushing her knee.

Her brilliant blue eyes went icy. "No. Not a second childhood. I just want to see … what I've been missing. I don't believe you're ever too old to explore new possibilities."

I watched her nipples harden even further in the stream of cold air, beginning to believe myself.

"Watch where you're going!" she yelled, grabbing the steering wheel and jerking it hard to the right.

The car leapt out of the path of an oncoming semi, just in time.

That should've taught me to keep my eyes on the road.

We stopped at a rest area just before Randsburg. Barbara had to use the can, and I was thirsty, among other things. Three hours cooped up with the good-looking lady had left me harder than Mount Whitney. I was thinking maybe I had time to get me some – quick and dirty, in and out and gone. No stopping.

I chugged a Red Bull and caught up with Barbara, from behind. She was staring off to the west, where somewhere in the parched, breathless distance lay the City of Angels, and a big, blue, beautiful ocean. I slid my hands around her narrow waist and pressed my hard-on up against her taut ass. "What say we grab us some exercise?" I breathed in her ear.

She went rigid, not looking back. I moved my sweaty hands over her stomach, up to her tits, gripping and squeezing the fleshy, low-slung pair. I kissed her neck, her funky choker, licked in behind her ear, my cock pressing hard and needy in between her rounded cheeks, my hands working her tits. She was hot, and I was on fire.

She spun around in my arms. "I don't want any ... commitments, Jay," she said, those blue eyes of hers blazing. "I'm free – for the first time in my life – and I want to stay that way. I'm going to see things, do things. I can't be tied down. I've got to keep moving."

"We'll do things, baby," I growled. "Hey, we're thinkin' along the same lines. I just want to fu– ... have some fun, is all. Not get married." I crushed her slim body against mine and kissed her. And she clutched my shoulders, kissed back.

There wasn't a soul around, just the crickets chirping away in the scrub, the sun glaring down, the dust kicking up every now and then. I pushed my tongue into Barbara's mouth and she pushed back. We swirled our slippery tongues together, my damp hands glued to her back.

She caught my tongue between her white teeth and sucked on it, pulled on it with her lips like she was sucking my cock. It drove me wild, and I grabbed onto her ponytails and ground my cock into her belly.

After flailing away with our tongues for a while longer, I gripped Barbara's bare legs and lifted her up, light as a feather. She coiled her legs around my waist and I carried her over to a picnic table, our mouths never breaking contact, her hot, sweet breath steaming into my face. I set her down on the end of the table, and we finally

44

did untangle our tongues, so she could pull her top out of her shorts and up over her head.

She was a rich, smooth, dark brown all over, and I held her by the shoulders and admired her for a moment – her full, hanging breasts, her fat, burnt-sugar nipples. She was twice as sexy as any girl half her age.

I grasped her bare breasts and squeezed, and her eyelids fluttered and she shivered. I bent my head down and licked at one of her swollen nipples, and she cried, "Yes!"

I thoroughly tongue-lashed her nipples, feeling the rubbery appendages stiffen, lengthen still more. I kneaded her hot tit-flesh as I licked at her buds, then sealed my lips around one thick nipple and sucked hard on it.

"Yes, baby! Yes!" Barbara groaned, leaning back, planting her hands on the sun-bleached wooden slats and urging me to feed on her chest.

I hungrily inhaled as much of her left tit as I could, tugged on it, then let it slide dripping wet out of my mouth. I devoured her other tit, pulled on it. Then I pushed her overripe melons together and bobbed my head back and forth between them, sucking and licking and biting her nipples, leaving them shining with my lust, achingly hard with hers.

She tore my T-shirt out of my jeans and pulled it over my head. I fumbled my belt and my fly open, shoved my jeans and shorts down, my cock springing up hard and yearning, vibrating in the buzzing air.

Barbara arched her body so that I could slide her shorts off, leaving her breathtakingly naked except for her boots. Her pussy was covered with springy, reddish-brown fur that glistened in the sunlight. I could smell her desire. I pushed her down onto the table and gripped her legs, felt up her firm thighs, kissed and licked her muscled

45

calves, my straining prick sniffing her downy pussy.

She cupped her splayed jugs and pinched and rolled her nipples, looking me in the eye and hissing, "Fuck me!"

I steered my fat hood into her damp bush, penetrating her slickness and plunging inside, grunting with satisfaction as her pussy lips gripped my shaft, hot and wet and silky. I started moving my hips, sliding my cock back and forth in her slit, motherfucking that sprawled-out fortysomething right out there in the open for all the world to see.

Barbara moaned, her body, her breasts bouncing in rhythm to my thrusting. I brushed her hands away and clutched at her tits, bending her legs backwards with my body, her boots riding my shoulders, pounding cock into her pussy. Sweat poured off my face and down onto hers.

I fucked that spectacular MILF faster and faster, pistoning away inside her, the sun scorching the two of us, the wet smack of our bodies slamming together filling the electrified air. She bit her fingernails into my arms and her mouth broke open in a silent scream. She stared blindly up at me, her slick, brown body quivering with all-out release.

"Fuck, yeah!" I bellowed, my cock exploding. I sprayed sizzling semen deep into Barbara's velvet cunt, hips flying, coming with a primal force I'd never experienced before, over and over.

When the frenzy finally ended, I leaned against the lady's legs, struggling to get my breath and my bearings back, gazing down into her smiling eyes.

She had to remind me what it was all about, saying, "Maybe we should hit the road, huh?"

We made it to Adelanto by ten, the time and the miles

flying by as I gushed all over Barbara like a teenager, all about my LA dreams. She listened, patiently and soothingly, like so many women before hadn't.

I pulled into the Pinewood Motel on the outskirts of town, buzzing with energy and excitement. We rented a shack of a cabin in a scraggly clump of trees that passed for a forest. And as soon as Barbara set her backpack down, I was all over her.

I gathered her in my arms and kissed her, babbling about how beautiful she was and lucky I was. She wriggled free, ran off into the bathroom, yelling behind her that she needed a shower and I needed to cool off.

But there was no way I was letting her escape that easily. I stripped off my clothes and then waited impatiently for the water to start running, for her to get nice and lathered up. Then I burst into the bathroom and tore the shower curtain aside, jumped into the tub with her. I greedily kissed her soft, moist lips, swallowing her protests, grabbing onto her slippery butt cheeks and squeezing, cock burning into her belly.

"I can't get rid of you, can I?" she said, when I finally let the both of us come up for air.

"Not a chance, Mrs Ferguson."

Her auburn hair was loose and wet about her shoulders. She looked even prettier that way, reminding me of a friend of my mother's when she'd come out of the water one hot summer day, dripping and wonderful, after swimming with us at our cottage.

We kissed some more, and our tongues collided. We frenched, the bathroom steaming up with the spray and our heat.

Barbara dropped to her knees. She captured my twitching cock in one hand and my tightened balls in the other, started stroking the one while squeezing the other. I

47

groaned and tilted my head back. Jerked my head back down when I felt her lips on my hood.

She popped my cockhead in and out of her warm, wet mouth, before sliding her lips over top of it and down. My cock glided into her mouth, and she began sucking on it with the practised skill of a knowing woman – no scraping or biting or gagging or spitting up. She took me down almost to the hairline, fingering my balls, tugging on my sac, then slowly pulled back, silky lips sliding up veined, pulsating shaft.

I rode her bobbing head with one hand and gripped the curtain railing with the other, the water splashing against my heaving chest and cascading down, Barbara wet-vaccing my cock. She reached up and played with my nipples, lightly raked her nails down my stomach, always sucking and sucking on my cock.

"Fuck that feels good!" I gasped, balls tingling and dick throbbing.

She suddenly grabbed my ass and jerked me forward, slamming cock all the way down her throat. I hung on for dear life, staring down at her staring up at me, my prick buried to the hilt in her mouth and throat.

She pulled back, and the pressure eased – a bit. Then she disgorged my cock, the meat oozing out of her mouth thick and raw and dripping. She left me quivering in front of her lips, before saying, "Fuck me up the ass!"

I pulled her to her feet, and she spun around and bent forward, facing the jetting water. I scooped up the soap and used it on my cock, her crack, then shoved my bloated hood up against her tiny pucker. She pressed her hands flat against the tiles, her arms shaking, as I punched my cap into her bum.

"Oh, God!" she whimpered.

I took hold of her waist and pushed forward,

squeezing my big, hard cock into her hot, tight opening, till my balls kissed the twin fleshy mounds of her violated bottom.

"Fuck me! Fuck my ass!" she screamed, twisting her head around, her face streaming.

I pumped that mature babe's gripping chute, slowly and surely, my body surging with sexual electricity. I moved faster, getting a good, hard, wicked rhythm going, sawing in and out of her ass.

She pushed back, matching my strokes perfectly. Like we were made for each other, meant for each other. Her bum rippled deliciously as we banged together, as I plunged deep inside her. Steam was everywhere, water flying all over the place. I desperately fucked Barbara's ass, knowing it was too good to last for too long.

She reached down between her legs and frantically rubbed her pussy. We were a well-oiled machine, my cock rocking back and forth in her vice-like butt, her fingers flying on her clit, our bodies shuddering with the impact of our ferocious lovemaking.

"I'm coming!" she screamed into the spray.

"I'm coming!" I hollered back, churning my hips in a frenzy.

She was jolted by brutal orgasm just as I was, dancing around on the end of my cock as she came and came and came, as I blasted torrents of come into her ass.

We lay together in the utter blackness, completely drained, only the whisper of an occasional car on the highway breaking the perfect, contented silence. She traced a fingertip over my chest, a nail around my nipples, and I hugged her close.

"Why don't we stay here awhile – get even better acquainted?" I said, softly kissing her hair.

Her finger stopped. She lifted her head off my chest, and I could feel her fever eyes on my face. I opened my mouth to say something more, but her finger pressed down on my lips, quieting me.

And when I woke up the next morning, she was gone. The note reading simply: "No stopping."

I've been searching for two weeks now. Aimlessly. Desperately. Up and down the blistering highways of Nevada and California and Arizona, back and forth over the dusty, sun-baked backroads. Searching for Barbara.

Everything else is on hold – my meetings with the movers and shakers of La-La Land, my ambitions, my momentum – until I find Barbara. I've just got to find that brown-haired beauty, you see, tell her what she really means to me. Convince her to slow down and give it a try – she and I.

My money's running low and I haven't slept in days. I've logged ten thousand miles and a hundred truck stops. But I've got to find her. I know she's just around the corner, waiting for me, wanting me.

Have you seen her?

The Stocks
by Roger Frank Selby

'Ah, there you are, Mr Finch.'

Finch lifted the plane from his work, mentally noting where the last shaving had been cut from the table leg he'd been squaring off for Smythe Minor, one of his less able students. He was glad his female visitor had chosen break time; his woodwork classes tended to be somewhat noisy and chaotic. A previous visit by the voluptuous drama teacher had generated anonymous embarrassing remarks and even wolf-whistles from the class. Unfortunately, he'd been unable to deal with the situation effectively until her glare and natural authority had silenced the room.

He brushed the shavings from his apron. 'What can I do for you, Miss Curzon?'

'I was wondering if you could make a prop needed for our forthcoming play?' She sounded slightly breathless.

'Just a single prop?' *Not hordes of swords and axes like you had me making last term?* 'Shouldn't be a problem. What is it exactly?'

'Well, it's quite a big item – a set of stocks, actually. You know, a sort of plank thing, holding one's head and hands …'

He immediately imagined the woman before him bent well over, her wrist and neck clamped in broad, polished

51

mahogany, her round backside raised high... Finch stopped his rampaging imagination when he found himself looking intently at her... She was blushing!

'What an interesting project. Do you have a drawing or picture I can work from?'

'Well no, Mr Finch ... Perhaps, you could sketch something?'

Finch grabbed his 2B pencil and flipped to a virgin page on his pad. He sketched rapidly, hearing her sharp intake of breath as the drawing of device and captive took shape. As a hard-up student, he'd made money on the streets of Paris and London from his swift artistry. He resisted the strong temptation to impart Miss Curzon's likeness on the captive wench. 'Is this what you have in mind?'

'Oh, Mr Finch! That's it – exactly!' She blushed again.

'Well, technically, this is a pillory. I believe stocks just hold the ankles when seated – but that would not be so suitable for the play, I'd imagine.'

'I agree ... The script does, actually call for "stocks" but I think I rather like the idea of being ... I mean, I had imagined something just as you have so ably drawn, and that would work far better with an audience, I should think.' The woman seemed to have come alive with that sketch, showing – not too explicitly – the vulnerability of one so captured.

'So, Miss Curzon, we'll continue to call our pillory "stocks" just in case some spoilsport makes me build ankle restraints instead?' He allowed himself a small grin.

'Quite!' She laughed into his eyes, then looked up as the bell rang. 'Oh dear, I have to go. Is that enough for you to get started?'

'What about the size of the thing. Is it for the seniors?

I could do with seeing the actor who's to fit in to it – make it bespoke for him … or her.'

'Must dash. Can I see you about that later?'

'After school?'

'Yes.'

She was late. She saw him through the corridor windows, lounging against his desk with his pad, sketching in the empty classroom. He cut a fine figure but always looked happier without his class. She knew he had trouble keeping order, sometimes. If only she could show him how she controlled a class. A matter of confidence, really.

But he also had this reputation of being something of an artist. She had seen one or two of his caricatures in the staffroom, and that sketch of 'stocks' and captive confirmed it. She wondered just what he was drawing now.

'Hello. So sorry I'm late.'

He closed his pad rather quickly. 'Hi. No problem.'

'Have you been doing some more sketching?' She lounged beside him, conscious of his height, maybe a little too close, as her breast brushed against the hairs of his bare forearm.

'I have.' He opened the pad at an early page, showing a drawing of an empty device.

'Wow! Look at all that detail. Hinges, clasps …'

'I'm assuming you want a robust, realistic device, with things working just as they should.'

'Absolutely.'

'And have you decided on the size?'

'Well,' she smiled, 'could you make it bespoke for me?'

He glanced at her, eyebrows raised.

She felt herself reddening again. 'Well, the lead actor

53

is just about my height …'

'No problem.' He straightened and faced her. 'Just lean your elbows on my desk for a start …'

She bent over and did just that, feeling the stiffening tips of her breasts jab the wooden surface.

'This gives us a general idea. I would guess that you probably want your back to be lower than that…'

'Shall I bend lower? Perhaps my wrist and neck should be close to desk level?' Her bosom flattened, spreading out against the ancient wood.

'Do you want your back to be horizontal then?' He rested his hand on the small of her back.

'Oh!' she jumped a little at his touch. The touch was not out of place in the circumstances, she decided. 'You mean level? Ah yes, that would be ideal.'

'It won't be very comfortable bent over that much with your legs straight.'

'Well, I would guess that comfort is not the idea of the device, besides, I'm quite flexible.'

She was. And she knew her bottom stood out quite nicely too. He pulled out a pocket tape measure and began taking measurements centred around her pose, muttering as he wrote them down on his sketchpad – how long and wide the base would have to be, the height of the neck and wrist holes and so on.

'Now, how wide apart do you want the wrists?'

She showed him.

'About a metre, then.' He came up close to her and carefully measured around her neck and wrists, presumably to work out the best diameter for the holes. Finally, he walked around to her side. She felt her heart give a lurch as he leant over and patted her bottom. 'That's it, thanks, Miss Curzon.'

For a second she considered objecting to the

familiarity, but she knew her bottom was sticking up quite outrageously and his touch had been so light and natural, almost thoughtless – an artist dismissing his model, perhaps.

'Oh, I'm sorry! I wasn't thinking …' He'd noticed her hesitation.

Her heart was still beating noticeably as she straightened. She decided she did not want to be dismissed. She raised her arms and stretched her shoulders. The natural action emphasised her jutting breasts and set his eyes on them. He quickly glanced down to the pad and his notes. Her eyes followed. 'Can I see some more of your sketches, please, Mr Finch?'

'I guess so, but …'

'Let me see.' She flipped over the pad pages and he didn't stop her.

This time his latest sketches showed an unmistakable Miss Curzon held captive. Several views – one from in front, her head slightly drooped and a view from the side and behind. He must have seen her in the swimming pool: his artist's eye saw how she would look in the raw, and here she was. They were roughly sketched nudes, however, outlines and details rather blurred but unmistakeably her – with her full breasts hanging down. He had them almost right.

She breathed in sharply. 'Oh!'

'I'm sorry if you're offended. I used to do figure drawing …'

'I can see that. But this is not from life, this is …'

'… just my imagination, unfortunately. Do you like them?'

She kept her eyes down on the drawing. She knew she was blushing yet again. 'I do, actually. They are marvellous.' Then she looked him in the eye. 'When did you last draw from life?'

He laughed, his eyes sparkling. 'It's been a few years.'

She didn't speak for a moment. 'A pity ... You are very good, in my humble opinion, but I expect it's pretty difficult finding a model?'

'There's the rub!' He grinned.

She closed the pad with a dismissive gesture. 'I know the sketches are strictly personal to you, but I'm a little worried about the students seeing these stocks being made. You know how they are about such things. *Their* imaginations will run riot!'

'I'll be doing the main assembly work out of hours. I can keep the project securely locked up in my storeroom.'

'Excellent! It's really very kind of you to do this for me Mr Finch ... When do you think they'll be ready?'

'I have all the wood I need in stock but some of the hardware I'll have to shop around for. Give me a week.'

It took him slightly longer, but the play wasn't for another month. She'd walked by his classroom after hours once or twice and seen the light coming from under the storeroom door. Then one day in the staffroom, he whispered discreetly, 'They're almost finished – just the varnish drying. After school tomorrow night?'

'Right.'

She chose a longish dress for her visit. Perhaps a rather similar one to the wench depicted in his first drawing. She found her breath coming more quickly as he led her straight into the spacious storeroom and closed the door.

There in the centre were the stocks – a sinister construction of polished mahogany and black wrought iron fittings, solid and stable on a low platform, a powerful icon of mediaeval punishment. Real hide cushioned the open neck and wrist slots. There was a sharp smell of wood, leather and varnish.

'Oh! They are quite beautiful, Mr Finch!'

'Would you like to try them for size, ma'am?' he smiled.

'Yes, I would.'

'Once I close them on you, you will be locked in and helpless, you do realise that, Miss Curzon?'

She knew that. That was precisely what excited her, 'But you will be here with me. Just promise that you won't leave me alone.'

'I can promise you faithfully that I will not leave you alone.'

She met his gaze and he held it. She felt her heart thumping.

She stood on the platform and bent her head low, placing her neck and wrist in the slots. He swung over the heavy top half of the board, carefully closing the lock. She found that her neck and wrists were loosely but securely held, while her view to the rear was cut off completely. The feeling was quite different to being bent over Mr Finch's desk. Her breasts touched no surface, but hung free, constrained only by her bra. Her bottom felt even more stuck out and exposed than before.

'Now you are my prisoner, Miss Curzon.' His voice was harder, with a certain relish.

'What are you going to do with me, Mr Finch?'

'First, I'm just going to sketch you.'

'Oh. With my clothes on?'

'Yes, briefly.'

Briefly? Her heart was pounding. 'Very well.'

After a minute or two out of sight, he showed her a drawing of herself bent over in the stocks – a helpless woman in a long summer dress, looking very vulnerable to the rear … Could her bottom look that big, she wondered?

Then he and the drawing vanished but she felt him behind her, his hands low on the outside of her legs, just under the hem of her dress.

'Oh!'

'Now I want to sketch you a little less draped. Is that OK?'

'How much "less draped"?' She breathed deeply.

'Tell me when to stop lifting your clothes – just say "when."'

With a shock, she noticed the mirror to her right. He already had her dress raised to her thighs. My God, he would soon discover …

She kept silent and he kept lifting – slowly, right over her bare bottom, past the dip of her naked waist. If he was surprised by the lack of knickers, he wasn't showing it. This man was an artist, she thought, completely at home with the female form. The dress was now up to her shoulder blades, revealing the tight, white brassiere strap. Had she been a less well-endowed woman, she would have forgone the bra too, but to jiggle about noticeably braless in school, even after-hours, would have been quite indiscreet.

He'd now lifted her clothes right up to her neck and forearms, revealing the sturdy cups of her brassiere, which, she could now see, gave a rather conical outline to their charges. She rather wished she hadn't worn it. Foolishly she tried to move her arms as if to reach around her back and unhook … Immediately, she felt the firm restriction of the hardwood surrounding the leather encircling her wrists.

'No "when", Miss Curzon?'

'No!' she laughed. 'Can you, ah, undo the strap for me? I really would like to be completely natural for your sketching.'

The woodwork master's heart was thumping as the full, splendid form of the drama teacher was revealed to his gaze. Her skin was so smooth. Not white, but creamy. Looking down on her back, he savoured the way the swell of her round behind narrowed into her waist and gently out again to her long back, the sight only marred by the strap across the groove of her spine.

Hardly trusting himself to speak, he unhooked her. On both sides of her back he could see the slightly whiter swell of her released breasts as he cleared the straps over her shoulders. He glanced in the mirror and saw how her tits had adopted a beautiful natural line as they hung lower in their fullness, the generous pink nipples pointing slightly forwards and outwards.

'Lovely!' he breathed.

'Thank you.'

'I'd like to clear away these clothes. Promise you won't run away if I release you for a moment?'

'I promise.'

She remained bent over in the stocks as he unlocked and lifted the top board to one side. She raised her neck and arms slightly as he pulled her clothes over her head. His hands made slight contact with the cool flesh of her breasts and they jiggled and swung with the movement. Soon, she was safely locked up again, quite naked in the stocks.

The sketching phase didn't last long. In a few minutes, he showed her the results. Excellent, of course, but she did not dwell on them, something more functional than mere sketching was on her mind. He must have noticed her preoccupation and seen the look in half-closed eyes, for he moved to her side and reached around and under her, boldly grasping a breast in each hand.

She sighed deeply. His touch was delicious. He soon gave up trying to play with both her breasts at the same time – they were more than a handful, even for his manly hands. His mouth joined in as he moved under her, sucking while his fingers squeezed and kneaded.

She looked in the mirror and watched him fondling her. But she also saw her bare bottom sticking out, unattended. He noticed her looking and she wiggled her waist and behind, suggestively.

With parting kisses on her nipples, he stood up beside her. His hand stroked down her back to the dip of her waist, then rose up smoothly, rounding over her bottom. His hand dallied there. He patted her right buttock. It was the lightest of smacks, yet it sent a dart of electricity through her loins. 'Oh!' He patted her left buttock – a trifle harder. No one had ever dared to do this to her before. 'Oh, Mr Finch!'

'You have only to say "stop", and I shall, Miss Curzon.'

She didn't trust herself to reply – but he had not asked a question, after all. A moment later, she felt his renewed touch on her bottom. His powerful, slightly rough, working hands were kneading the flesh of her bottom instead of her breast, opening and closing her buttocks, imparting the occasional firm slap. In response, she found herself wiggling her bare arse from side to side.

He began to spank her, fairly hard.

She cried out a little with each loud smack, discovering that quite a loud smack hardly hurt at all, but made her breath come quicker and her heart beat faster.

Sometimes the spanking would pause and his hand would stray between her legs, then trail up delightfully through her moist lips.

'I am your prisoner,' she breathed, 'you can do with me as you will.' A little over-dramatic perhaps, but she had already seen that his trousers were fit to burst their straining contents.

He took them off.

She was not displeased with the side view of him in the mirror: a magnificent member raised in salute to her naked body. She wanted to be closer to him. 'Please bring him around to the front for a moment, Mr Finch.'

It was an order. She had her bossy voice on, but he was happy to come around to where she could eyeball his cock directly. He saw her hands convulse slightly as she went to hold him and found her wrists constrained once again by the leather padding.

'Can you release me again, please – just briefly?'

He opened the stocks. Her hands came together to hold him firmly and to guide the swollen head into her mouth. He gasped, feeling the sweet, wet warmth of her mouth as she took him in. He lifted her a little from the wooden slots, reaching again for her creamy, swinging breasts as she now took her turn at sucking.

It was difficult to say how long she sucked him – certainly longer than he had sucked her breasts – but he was surprised and slightly shocked with the skill of her tongue around his cockhead and the way her hands played along his shaft, lifted and fondled his balls and even felt around his bottom. He was more than ready for her, and even in danger of culminating his performance when she finally released him.

'Now, Mr Finch, lock me down and come up behind

me.'

That bossy voice again.

'I'm locking you down, but *I'll* decide what happens from now on.'

Her silence was eloquent.

Maybe he'd hurt her feelings but the tone of his voice had done the trick. Behind her again, he gave her one or two more spanks for good measure.

'Oh!'

Then he spread her cheeks wide. Her wet lips opened a little and he guided himself into her.

'Aaaahhhh!'

Most of the sigh came from her, but he joined in a little too, as he felt himself slip deep up inside her tightness.

He slowly slid in and out of her.

He took his time. He held onto her waist but also stroked her wide hips and buttocks, spanking them alternately as she rolled her penetrated pussy around his penetrating member, very gentle and easy fucking to start with, apart from the smacks.

This was what she had been craving – the intimacy with Mr Finch and the forced submission of the stocks. To her surprise, both had measured up superbly! With her head held down and her hind quarters free, she allowed her bottom to toss around wildly while the spearing cock moved inside her, now slow and steady, now pistoning fast, right up to the hilt, flattening her labia at the end of each deep stroke. With her knees bent forward a little and her thighs slightly apart, she was wide open for him, a direct line from the root of his crotch into the depths of her belly

She felt her excitement build and build with the hard

thrusting, felt herself beginning to tighten around him, knowing he would be feeling her squeezing him along his length. She began to cry out, to howl, her bottom seeming to come alive, rolling and thrusting against him. He was crying out too, holding onto her waist, his motion even more urgent as the long strokes of his hips began to deliver his body's purpose deep within her body.

He lasted a long time, filling her, pulling on her creamy buttocks to bounce and quiver, hard up against him, again and again.

They were still for a long time afterwards, locked together, basking in the afterglow.

'Oh, Mr Finch … That was so … so lovely!'

There was less noise in the class these days and the quality of work had improved noticeably. He saw her tap on the glass in the corridor and motioned her inside the door. There she waited, her hands behind her back on the door knob, unconsciously emphasising her impressive bosom. She looked absolutely radiant these days. One of the boys attempted a wolf whistle but Mr Finch's swift scowl at the culprit nipped it in the bud.

'OK you lot, get on with your work.'

They did.

At his desk, the two teachers could talk business.

'Mr Finch, I was wondering if you would be interested in constructing another major prop for our next play – it's set on the quarterdeck of an old ship. Specifically I need a ship's wheel.'

'Right.'

He sat down, opened his pad and started sketching a detailed ship's wheel as she looked over his shoulder.

'Hmmmm – how big would that be? Can you draw in a person to give it scale?'

He sketched again. The naked woman was bent low over the wheel, arms lashed to the spokes, her heavy breasts hanging down, her bottom offered up.

She lowered her voice and spoke close to his ear. 'Perfect! That's exactly how I want it.'

E620
by Lucy Felthouse

Morning lectures are a bitch. No matter how much sleep I get the night before – whether it be the recommended eight hours, or an excessive ten – I still cannot get to grips with mornings. I've just come to accept that I'm far from being an early bird, and always stop at the University shop for a can of Red Bull before continuing up to room E620. I then saunter in, half-asleep and grin weakly at my classmates and lecturer before slumping into a chair and popping open my can.

Today is no exception. Although I'm not bored, or particularly tired, I still feel myself dozing off. Aware of how bad this would look if the lecturer noticed, I decide to do something to spice up the atmosphere a little. I let my mind wander, not even telling it off when it hesitates outside the door marked 'XXX.'

I chuckle inwardly at its boldness, particularly this early in the day, and my consciousness takes this to be the nod, and we're in. Welcome to the naughty part of my brain, probably the largest part, and certainly not a place for the faint-hearted! A mischievous little character wanders up and down the aisles of my 'X' files, and finally re-appears, carrying a box marked 'favourite fantasies'. Ah, he chooses well.

Back in the real world, I catch Karl's eye across the room. He grins, and I suspect his creative mind is up to mischief, not unlike mine. Funny really that it should be Karl. Perhaps he sensed he was in my thoughts. More specifically the box marked 'favourite fantasies'.

Karl is – to borrow the cliché – "the one that got away". Our relationship exists purely in erotic daydreams, safe from the prying eyes of the outside world, and safe from rejection.

My entry into the world of erotic literature has plenty to do with Karl's interference. We were chatting one lunchtime, about sex in general, funny stories and so on. He then suddenly came out with,

"You should write porn!"

"What!" I said, shocked.

"You should. You're one of the most open-minded women I've ever met, you should have a bash at writing something. I reckon you'd be really good."

I didn't think much of it at first, and soon forgot about the conversation. Karl, however, refused to let it go and kept bringing it up, then eventually he dared me to write something. I relented, and asked him what his favourite sexual fantasy was. He told me the gist; every teenage boy's fantasy, having sex with his young and attractive teacher. I wrote my first piece of erotic fiction based on that. Needless to say, he read and thoroughly enjoyed the story, and encouraged me to write more erotica, then gave me feedback on what I'd written. From those lunchtime chats, we developed an insight into each other's sexual tastes.

The fantasy I'm thinking of right now takes place in this very room, E620. As you walk in, you're standing in a slight alcove, then the room opens out to tables, chairs, and a seldom used overhead projector. The door has a sturdy-looking Yale lock, the type you can lock from inside without the key.

In my fantasy, I'm looking fab in a knee-length black skirt, black patterned stockings, knee-high boots and a chunky jumper. It's winter, for God's sake!

Karl's looking damn fine in faded light blue jeans. Tight, of course, clinging to his ass and thighs. His black T-shirt emphasises his broad chest and muscular arms. His sexy tattoos, always an element of fascination for me, are clearly visible on his right arm, one encircling his bicep, the other adorning his inner forearm.

So there we are, both looking good enough to eat, in our morning lecture. We unintentionally keep making eye contact, and smile at each other as we glance away, embarrassed.

Not so embarrassed that I don't look again, however, and this time he's yawning and stretching, his T-shirt has risen enough to give me some pleasant eye candy. I slip my phone out of my bag and send him a text:

"R u thinkin wot I'm thinkin?"

His reply:

"Yeah, I'm horny as fuck!"

"That's not wot I meant, u were yawnin!"

"Yeah but u look sexy 2day, ur distractin me!"

The banter continues throughout the lecture, as it always has, all mouth, no action.

Lunchtime arrives, and the class files out in dribs and drabs and I notice Karl's making a right old song and dance about putting his stuff in his bag. Finally he stands up, bag in one hand, his empty coffee cup in the other. We walk to the door, and he throws the cup in the bin, pushes the door closed and flips the latch.

"What ya doin?"

I ask, already half knowing the answer, but not quite letting myself believe it. Karl drops his bag to the floor, and holds his hand out for mine. I pass it to him, and they lie abandoned by the door.

Within seconds, they are forgotten as we look at each other, this moment so frequently thought of, but neither of us ever knew what would happen next, or ever thought we'd find out.

There had always been something stopping us getting it together before. It certainly wasn't a lack of chemistry! Our friendship was just a friendship, but strong sexual attraction and mutual admiration has long bubbled away underneath.

Months of flirting, talking about sex, and discussing my dirty stories in fine detail have finally come to a head. Suddenly, in a classroom, we're kissing. Karl's tongue is in my mouth, his full lips pressed against mine. It's such a hungry kiss I'm taken aback; mind you, it had been building up for so long it's hardly surprising.

My hands are currently very confused. Being presented with this wonderful gift, they're unsure where to grope first. So I settle for one hand on his arse, and the other playing with the mop of curls at the nape of his neck. The cleverly placed hand on his arse enables me to pull him closer, and I feel his hard-on against my groin. I groan inwardly, my pussy positively drooling. My pants are stuck to me, but I'm in such a state of bliss, I couldn't really care less.

Now, one advantage of having Karl read my dirty stories is that he knows what kind of sex I like. A second advantage is his feedback, which hints at what kind he likes. In fact, we've talked about it so often, and in such great detail, sometimes I feel like we've already done it!

I tug his hair gently, rendering his throat exposed. I pounce, covering the sensitive skin with alternating butterfly kisses, tiny nips, and sensual sucks – giving him a taste of what's to come.

I feel like I'm going to go crazy. My mind is a tumult of emotions. On the one hand, I want to savour this as long as possible, exploring every inch of his naked skin. But on the other hand, I'm so horny I want his cock deep inside me, fucking me long and hard, making me come all over his balls, while filling me full of his hot spunk. Even kinkier, he'd then pull out, and shove his cock in my mouth so I could taste our combined juices. Satisfied he was clean, he'd go down on me and lick me clean, saving just a little bit in his mouth to kiss me again.

The decision is taken out of my hands. Karl takes my wrists and guides me backwards until the back of my thighs hit a table. He continues to push, so I hop onto the table, my feet dangling in mid-air. Grinning filthily at me, he slowly pulls off his T-shirt. I feel my heart skip a beat as the muscular body I've so long envisioned is revealed to me.

I attempt to stand, so I can reach out for him once more, but he forces me back onto the table. His body covers mine; his arms restraining mine, his lips covering mine, his groin exciting mine.

I'm getting to the point of no return, where any control is lost, and my lust takes over. We continue kissing, and he relaxes his hold on my arms. I take the opportunity to reach down and undo the button and fly on his jeans. I slide my hand into the gap I've made, find his erect penis and feel myself getting wetter as I stroke it.

It's incredibly hot and hard, and I tremble inside as I envisage it thrusting inside me, filling my wet hole. I close my eyes as I caress his cock. I increase the pace, and Karl moans, a deep guttural noise that makes my clitoris throb in response. I love that he's horny, and I know exactly what will make him want me even more.

I remove my hand from his jeans and get off the table.

69

I guide him so he's in my place, his buttocks against the table, his erection straining against the pale blue denim covering his groin. Not for long though, as I grasp the loopholes at his waist and pull, revealing his tight white boxer shorts. Within seconds, they're down too, revealing his proud prick, standing long and thick from his tangle of pubic hair.

Without hesitation, I drop to my knees. I reach out and grasp his twitching erection, holding it firm in one hand as my mouth draws closer to its smooth head, which is already gleaming with his juices. I stick out my tongue to taste his precum, then sliding my tongue along the length, my lips curve into a grin as he gasps at the contact.

I pull back and blow on the dampened skin, then suddenly lunge forward and slide my lips over the head once more, this time taking his cock fully into my mouth, as far as it will go. I suck and squeeze him with my lips and tongue – his moans of delight heightening my arousal.

I suck him with enthusiasm, loving the feeling of control I'm getting. Although it's me on my knees, I know damn well he's putty in my hands, or more literally, my mouth.

I use my free hand to stroke his balls and perineum, the combined techniques guaranteed to drive him wild. I can feel his dick becoming harder as though he's ready to come, so I slow my pace. I'm not going to let him … yet. I give his erection a final lingering lick as I make my way back up his body, kissing, nibbling and sucking my way to his lips, which are curved up in a smile.

"That was …"

I cut him off with a kiss, sliding my tongue into his mouth, allowing him to taste himself on my tongue and lips. He deepens the kiss, sliding his arms around my waist and pulling me close. I relax into the embrace, feeling like I'm walking on air. I simply cannot wait any longer for him to touch me. I grab one of his wrists from behind my back and place it on my breast.

He gently cups and caresses the soft flesh through my clothes, then suddenly his hand heads south, under my layers and up again so he's touching my bare skin. The temperature down below raises a few degrees, and I can feel the dampness in my pants increase. I don't think I'm going to last much longer. There's a feeling of desperation running throughout my entire body, desperation to have his cock inside me, screwing me long and hard … making me come until it hurts.

He fingers my nipple, quickly making it erect and then pinching the tender flesh, making me squeal a little. He pulls off my jumper, giving him full access to my naked flesh, tormenting my breasts and nipples, sucking, licking, biting. The feel of his teeth against my skin is driving me crazy, like a red hot fire blazing its trail south.

I push one of his hands down, leaving him to take the hint. He does, thank god. He lifts up the hem of my skirt, his hands roaming over my smooth thighs above my stocking tops. I open my legs a little to give him better access. His fingers creep under my pants to explore my vulva, stroking along the swollen folds of flesh, then dipping between them to see what an effect he's had on me. The love juices flow so freely, he stops teasing my nipple and orders me back onto the table, but not before removing my underwear.

He parts my legs, presenting him with a full view of my engorged flesh. Suddenly his face disappears from view and I throw my head back in ecstasy as he tongues my clit. Karl licks my outer labia, his stubble grazing my smooth skin, giving a contrasting sensation from the

71

warm tenderness of his tongue. He dips into the wetness in the middle, lapping up all the juices he's caused me to secrete. He thrusts his tongue in and out of my pussy, reaching in as far as he can go, stimulating all the sensitive nerve endings and accelerating me towards a crashing climax.

I tangle my hands in his hair, unwilling to give him the chance to stop. I'm so close to coming now, I'm moaning and thrashing around, arching my back. Just as I can feel the familiar feeling start to emanate throughout my body, he stops. Just as I'm registering disappointment, he takes my clit between his lips and sucks. That's it. The tingling feeling spreads, my vaginal walls contract, and the floodgates open. I moan loudly as the come soaks my inner thighs, all the while Karl is lapping away, tasting my love juices.

The pulsations have barely died away when Karl stands, his still erect penis looking fit to burst. He enters my wet warmth in one motion, triggering a new set of contractions to ripple through my groin. We both moan at the sensation and he doesn't move for a moment. We relish the feeling, I of being filled, he of being surrounded. Then he moves inside me. The sensitivity is intense and I simply allow him to have his way. I lean back slightly and wrap my legs around his back, pulling him deeper into me.

He pounds into me deeply and violently, grasping my thighs hard for leverage, leaving marks on the pale skin. I know I'm going to have bruises in a couple of days, but I don't care, I figure it'll be a sexy reminder. He moves rhythmically in and out of me, coating his cock in my juices which are increasing rapidly.

I dig my nails into his arms as he fucks me, and bite his neck and chest to muffle the noises I'm making. I want to scream, but somehow having to keep the noise down is making the whole experience more exciting. It's so dangerous and naughty. We're fucking in a classroom. We've been taught in this room for almost three years. We've flirted and talked dirty in this room for almost three years. And now he's sending me over the edge in this room, the atmosphere thick with lust.

My limbs clutch him desperately, hardly believing that this is finally happening. He's driving his hard cock deep inside my soaking wet, red-hot cunt. He slows down momentarily, almost as though he's running out of steam. Seconds later, I breathe a sigh of relief as he ups the pace once more.

Only this time, it's different. He's not just upping the speed, he's upping the intensity. He's thrusting into me now with an animal ferocity, his thighs audibly slapping against my ass. He leans down to me, his arms moving up my back to my shoulders, and as he pulls me on to him, he kisses me longingly and deeply. It's obvious he's getting close now – he seems to be lost in his passion. He slows once more, gyrating against me, creating delicious friction on the delicate nub of flesh nestling between my thighs. He applies slightly more pressure and I dig my nails into his biceps as I feel myself contracting around his cock once more. He begins to fuck me like a man possessed, fast, hard and wild. My orgasm intensifies and lengthens as he continues to torment me.

Finally, my spasms are matched by his. I feel his cock starting to throb and twitch inside me. Pounding into me one last time, he pulls out with a sexy groan and fires his load all over my hungry nether mouth. The sensation is fucking incredible. His come is so hot I feel like it could almost burn me.

As the last of his orgasm wanes, he collapses against

me, spent. Months of agonising flirting and fantasising, and boy was it worth it. Karl raises his head from its position on my chest and looks at me, his face flushed, eyes bright. He leans up for another kiss, and I'm just thinking maybe we're going to go again when there's a noise outside.

Someone tries the door. It's locked.

There's a sharp irritated knocking … For Christ's sake, FUCK OFF, I think. A little privacy here. Then I giggle. We're in a classroom, how can we expect privacy?

The knocking comes again. Then someone calling my name. Repeatedly. More knocking.

Suddenly I realise someone is intruding on my private territory. They're trying to get inside my head and coax me out, and, DAMN IT, they've succeeded. I come back to earth with a bump.

Karl's standing in front of me grinning, waving his hands in front of my face.

"Where the hell have you been? I've been trying to get your attention for five minutes, everyone else has gone! Must have been a good daydream."

Crush
by Primula Bond

'You've probably got something exciting going on tonight, Polly –'

Polly glances up from her perch in the corner of the show room. It's a cinch, this job. First one she's had since leaving school. This guy Giles pays her to sit there all day, looking pretty, typing out price lists, enticing passing trade to come in from the cold and view the latest exhibition. Sometimes even selling a picture.

All because she'd done a nude sitting for one of the gallery's artists and shuffled in one day looking for payment. The artist wasn't there, but the painting was. Hanging right up there on the wall, in fact, lit bright with a baby spot. In strong, brutal sweeps of flesh and chalky white oils he'd depicted her sprawled across a plain wooden floor, arms out, spine arched, legs open, knees collapsed, hair thrown across her face, looking as if she'd just been fucked.

Which she hadn't, yet. Oh, got close, you know, with fingers and tongues. Even had a girlie session once or twice after clubbing with a very sexy, very persistent French exchange student which was pretty wild. But she'd never sat on a cock. She'd acted it for the artist, faked it, posed it.

But she'd never had a guy's cock pushing into her and making her scream with pleasure.

Giles was in the gallery that day. He'd given her the money, glanced at the painting and back at her. Never said a word. She was swathed in black tights and boots and a big old scarf that day so maybe he didn't put two and two together. But there was something in the way his solemn amber eyes studied her, seemed to look right through to her bones, that made her feel very young and totally naked.

And obviously something about her made him offer her the job. He might have ignored her ever since, and she should probably be out there looking for something better, but she never wants to leave.

Her body goes hot, like central heating, and she tries not to wriggle on the hard little chair like a naughty schoolgirl needing a wee.

'No. Nothing exciting tonight. Why?'

Giles straightens a picture and stares out of the window. 'Valentine's Day?'

Polly blushes harder and bends her head over the computer to hide it. ' No boyfriend.' She bites on a biro. 'No Valentine.'

Giles strokes his chin. There's always a rough dark shadow there, like he's permanently holding a piratical beard at bay. He's so sophisticated, so smooth and sorted on the surface, but those bristles mean there's something about him needs taming. She wonders if he has a hairy chest. How warm his stomach is under those loose linen shirts. Today's there's a tantalising strip of brown skin where a button has come undone. What his legs are like under those cool loose jeans. What it would feel like to kiss an older guy.

'Great,' he says quietly. 'So can you help out at the party this evening?'

His hand dives into his pocket. Polly stares where his

hand has gone. Straight at his crotch, in fact. It's rude, but no ruder than a man staring at a girl's tits. It was the same with the music master at school. He was the only man in the convent, apart from the priest. All the girls thought about was what their cocks looked like under their clothes.

He's pulling out a wad of notes. She tries to pick a stray hair from the corner of her mouth. She's still trying to detect a bulge behind his fly, thinks she can see one. But hell, why on earth would he be getting hard from standing here talking to little old her?

'I'll make it worth your while!' He leans over, hooks his finger against her cheek, draws the offending hair out of her mouth. A single tiny drop of saliva pings off it like a diamond. Then he lays some crisp tenners down neatly on her desk. 'Just make sure you look stunning tonight. We've got lots of press coming.'

He winks at her. Her stomach flips. Then he's gone.

Because to him she's just a kid. And he has a girlfriend. Well, woman friend. She swaggers in to the gallery nearly every day. Checking up on him? She wears bizarre leather trousers, thinks she's Chrissie Hynde. She's elegant, though, black hair smooth like a helmet, and she's called Lady Henrietta. She always pauses in front of Polly's desk, barks out some question about Giles, never looks her in the eye.

She's here right now, twitching in his chaotic office down in the basement, spiky heels kicking impatiently at the air while he dares to deal with his minions, sipping the strong black coffee Polly makes for her.

Polly's the one who stands in the gallery doorway in her long dresses, bed hair piled up messily, black fingernails beckoning in the punters. But Henrietta's the one who looks like a hooker.

The artist responsible for painting her in the nude comes down the spiral staircase from the upper landing where he's been hanging the last paintings for tonight's private view.

'Can't take your eyes off him, can you, duck? Giles is the most handsome hetero art dealer in London!' he teases, waggling his hammer at her. 'So. Got a crush?'

'Nah. Far too old!' Polly tosses her hair. She wanders across the highly polished floor to re-arrange the lilies in the window. 'And he's got Lady Henrietta, anyway.'

'He's my age I'll have you know, young lady! And as for her, that's no love affair. They look good together, that's all. Kind of risqué and rackety. They use each other for publicity. And sex.'

Polly's stomach tightens with jealousy. Sex, the word, everything to do with it, hangs in the cool air like heavy perfume.

'Do you think they're doing it right now?' She fiddles with the catalogues just back from the printers, smelling headily of glossy paper.

'Doing what?'

'You know. It. In his office.'

'Fucking, do you mean, Polly Pocket?'

Her armpits are prickling, and the backs of her hands. She presses her thighs together, increasing the throbbing deep in her pussy. 'Yeah.' Her voice is a croak.

A smart couple open the door, letting in the bitter wind. Polly paints on a greeting smile. Then, downstairs, Henrietta and Giles start shouting. The punters scuttle away.

'What's going on?'

'Told you they weren't all that.' The artist shrugs in the direction of the argument. 'Perhaps fighting fires them up.'

78

Henrietta's voice grows louder, as if someone has turned up the volume. 'She's splayed naked all over the walls, and now you want her handing the drinks round to the critics tonight?'

'It's art, Henrietta, and she has a body to die for. They'll lap it up! They'll be queuing up to lap *her* up-'

'Don't be disgusting!'

'You're the one obsessing about her!' Giles is slamming the drawers of his desk. 'But what's any of this got to do with you? This is *my* gallery, not yours. And she's no tart. You can tell she's still a virgin –'

'So? That just makes her all the more tempting!'

Polly is hanging over the banisters as the voices descend into angry muttering.

'How the fuck does he know –'

'That you're a virgin?' The artist tucks her hair behind her ear and pads back up the spiral staircase. 'It's in the eyes, girl. We all know.'

'How many times have I told you?' Now Giles is chasing Henrietta up the stairs. 'You haven't been invited!'

'I'm not bloody Cinderella, you know!' Henrietta trips over her pointed toe as she gets to the top step. 'I'm just as entitled to go the Berkeley Square Ball as you!'

'Yes, darling, of course you are. Pumpkin, glass slipper and all.' Giles swipes his hand over the top of his head. 'But what would your bloody husband think about that?'

Henrietta staggers against Polly's desk, knocking over her vase of white carnations. Water seeps across a pile of typing. Henrietta just glares, an aristocratic flush streaking angrily across her cheek bones. The kind of hectic colour you might get after a good day's fox hunting. It even stains the bridge of her hooked nose, as if someone has punched her.

'Not in front of the staff, Giles!'

'So now you know, Polly. Lady Henrietta's married. But not to me. I've a double ticket but I can't take her to the Berkeley Square bloody Ball, with royalty and Mick Jagger and God knows who else parading about. I've a reputation to keep up.'

'Oh, right. The suave bachelor.' The artist titters from up above.

'Gigolo, more like!' Henrietta is still glaring at Polly.

The onset of a terrible giggle fit crowds inside Polly's chest. The kind that attacks you in church or on a crowded tube.

'Royalty?' She asks Giles, as if it's just the two of them. 'Mick Jagger?'

'So let the suave bachelor take his *unmarried* little virgin to the ball.'

Henrietta stalks past Polly in a rage and hauls open the street door, expecting someone to scurry after her. But everyone just turns back to their work.

Into the reverberating awkward silence Polly hears herself say, 'I'll go with you, Giles.'

Giles is halfway back down to the basement. 'You must be joking, Polly,' he sighs. 'You're young enough to be my daughter.'

Polly is still young enough to be crushed by that remark. He barely notices her. Thinks she's no better than jail bait – and not in a good way.

She catches the artist's eye and he blows her a kiss. 'I'll take you shopping, Pocket. The guy's blind! We'll show him what you're offering on a plate. You'd look edible in a bin bag, but I'm thinking Holly Golilightly meets Belle de Jour. Let's knock his bloody Fair Isle socks off.'

In sculpted black dress, killer heels, and hair tortured into a complicated pleat, Polly thinks she looks more like Edith Piaf turning tricks, but what the hell. She's going to *make* Giles notice her. So what if she's meant to be invisible, just handing round drinks and nibbles? She'll do all that, but she'll make him see her in a whole new light as well.

'And the model? For that picture?' A fat man with pocked skin points at the picture of her, running his sweaty fingers up the glass, up her painted splayed legs, towards the shadow of her painted pussy. 'I thought the artist was gay, but it looks like he's shagged this little slut senseless.'

Polly opens her mouth to put him straight, feels the scarlet lipstick parting stickily, but just then she sees Giles staring at her across the expensive crowd of style gurus and arts editors. He makes a drinking gesture and she scuttles over with her tray to his circle of posh mates and clients. The men look her over, their eyes watering. The women purse their lips. Polly feels a surge of power, knowing that the Herve Leger dress clings to every curve, pushes her big, plump breasts up and out. That the whole *ensemble* has transformed her into a vamp.

Every time she glances up, Giles is watching her. But she can't read his face.

'How are the pictures selling?' She sidles up to him towards the end of the party, tipsy from all the dregs she's drained downstairs. He's by the window, saying goodbye.

'Good, Polly, thanks to you.' He turns to her. 'They've been round you like bees round a honey pot. There's going to be an auction for that painting.'

'Wow. Fame at last!' She licks her lips. 'Except no-one will have recognised me.'

'Oh, but they could all tell it was you!' He grins at her. He's shaved, she notices. Smooth, but still shadowy. Smells of some delicious aftershave. White shirt whiter against his dark skin. 'That dress makes you look naked.'

Her pussy goes hot and tight. But it's not sleazy, what he's said. Just sexy. Really, really sexy.

'Just going to start the washing up,' she murmurs, aware of her knees knocking as she totters down to the basement. 'Have to get going.'

In the office she glugs a huge glass of Frascati. There's no dishwasher. Just a tray of kiss stained glasses, his desk and cabinets, and the sink. She has to bend over to scrub. She kicks the shoes off. The Frascati fizzes pleasantly in her head. She rubs herself against the edge of the work surface. Giles had imagined her naked …

'Thanks for your help, Polly.'

Upstairs a few feet are scraping goodbye across the floor. Presumably the artist is seeing them out. Because Giles is in here, with her.

'That's OK. You're paying me, remember?'

'I couldn't take my eyes off you tonight.'

She can hardly breathe. 'You told me to look good.'

She plunges her hands into the soapy water. And Giles plunges his hand up her skirt.

Polly squeals loudly, and breaks into a sweat. All that washing up. All that standing and talking upstairs under the spotlights. All that smiling. The wine. The desperate wanting. And now Giles's hand sliding up her bare thighs, stroking against her knickers, feeling the ready wetness.

People are deflowered on wedding nights, in bike sheds, teenage bedrooms, hay barns, car seats, woods, dim alleys. There's cider, puddles, coat cupboards, sofas, carpets, mud. Usually in the dark. Always in a hurry.

For Polly it's none of those places. But her

deflowering *is* in a hurry. There are people about. People waiting around. The door is open. The minute he touches her she wants it. Him. All of him. She holds herself very still, bent over the sink, not sure what to do. She relishes the waiting. His touch is barely there. Maybe waiting for her to slap him away. Tension crackles in the silent room. Pure tension, physical enough to touch. No mess of noise and words.

Giles knows where to go. Just one finger drawing a line down the hidden damp crack as if measuring her. Oh God, she wants him to like her! That finger becomes him, warm, hard, stroking, pushing. She bends lower over the washing up, her dress riding up tight, releasing the strong female scent of her arousal. She can't turn round. Too shy. If she turns round, what does she do? Smile? Kiss him? Say something dirty? Scream?

Her bottom knows, though. It lifts, pushes against him, his trousers, and now she can feel it in there, the real thing. His cock. She's seen them before. Touched them. Even licked one. This one is hard and pushing between her legs. His finger is inside her knickers now, picking at the seam ready for her to come loose.

He pushes his finger right inside her and pulls her away from the sink. Hooks her away, finger still up there. He kicks at the door, and his finger slides out, coated with her wetness. She wants it inside her again, to push in harder this time, the urge as violent and natural as the urge to piss, or punch.

He looks so good in the gleam of one dull light bulb. His face is craggy and handsome and totally focussed on her. His arms are strong. He glances past her. Maybe changing his mind, because she's young enough to be his daughter. The door isn't closed properly.

The bright lights of the gallery intrude. Their feet are

skidding about on the wet floor. He makes a groaning sound. Polly presses against him, ready to kiss him, that would be good. Her skirt is up round her hips, too tight to pull down. She still has on the rubber gloves, and is too young to see the funny side. They look stupid. She puts them round his neck, still pressing urgently against him, afraid he might stop, but he isn't going to stop. He presses his mouth onto hers, more his teeth really, hard against her, still groaning as he pushes her hard against the sink, the edge of it jabbing into her spine, and her legs fall open. He bends his knees, thrusts himself up between her thighs, lifting and grinding, and her legs open further.

Polly wrenches the gloves off. She scrabbles at his trousers but the buckle won't undo. He's pushing his fingers up inside her again and when he puts his mouth on her neck, under her hair where it's falling out of the pins, she goes weak and moans.

'Oh Christ,' he groans in response, pulling her face round to face him. He looks rumpled, and troubled, and glazed with desire. 'I can't believe it, that's all – you're so young and gorgeous –'

The words are thrilling and he starts kissing her, really hard. His lips and teeth are brutal. She sucks on his tongue when it slips inside her mouth, so unused to all this wetness but it's mind-blowing, and he can tell because he pushes his tongue in harder, making it feel like fucking, and her cunt squeezes tight with excitement.

'Be my Valentine, Giles,' she whispers, female power surging through her. 'Do it to me.'

He groans again and hoists her up onto his scuffed desk where the trays of glasses are waiting to be washed. And where she's left his Valentine Card. He pushes everything aside. Something rips and splinters. Something else falls to the floor and smashes. Surely someone will hear? But then she's on her back, the wooden surface hard but wet and soapy too against her shoulder blades. The bare parts of her, her bottom, back and thighs, squeak and slither.

Then Giles has her knickers off.

Polly closes her eyes, suddenly shy to look at his face. But that invites in images of him with Henrietta. Smooth operator, ripping knickers off with one hand. He must have done it millions of times. Henrietta lying here, smooth operator as well, arching and grinding about on the desk, not just falling back and waiting for him to do it, she'd be doing things to him, crushing him between her thighs, knowing exactly what to do with her hands, her mouth, her pussy goddamit. How exactly to please him. What the fuck does Polly know?

Her legs look long and white in the sickly light. She opens them, grips Giles round the hips as he kneels over her. Giles is her man now, touching her, lifting her, kissing her, wrenching open his own trousers, flicking the belt out of the loops and cracking it like a whip. They smile briefly at the sound, then kiss again, more tender and knowing, less teeth, more tongues this time, the taste of red wine.

She wants his cock now, she wants to see it and touch it, but he's all shirt tails and flapping tuxedo. Everything is so new. His smell, Christ, his maleness. The rough fabric of his clothes. The muscles in his arms. She tries to see herself in a soft focus movie, hopes he'll see her moving in a beautiful sex scene.

He puts his hand down and there it is, a warm blunt thing nudging, edging inside, ridiculously cosy warm at first, but harder as it slides in, not nudging now but shoving. Her wetness makes it easy, her body opening to let it in. She waits for it to hurt. For there to be blood.

Embarrassment. But she is so desperate to have him in there, it's all she wants, why feel bad about something as heavenly as this? She wraps her legs tight round him as his cock thrusts in possessively. If there's any sensation when he pierces her it's as delicious as popping a champagne cork. Popping your cherry. Her cherry. It's done. She grips with muscles she never knew she had inside her, and they are off.

At least, that's what Henrietta might say. Maybe she'd buck and whoop and smack his belt down to bring red stripes out on his flanks while she cried 'tally ho!' She's heard that people like being smacked. She's sure Henrietta would love smacking.

Whatever. It's just Poppy and Giles right now, and this is like being in the centre of a storm. She's half active, half passive. Half out of her body, half flailing about inside it. Fucking is more effort than she imagined it would be. Those sex scenes are all slow motion, all tracking shots of flesh and hip and nipple. This is heaving and poking and pointing and panting. It's hard work, but mostly for him.

She wants to keep quiet. She's not a screamer. Except a year or so later, in a hot dry tent in an open field, she'll scream as she's fucked because she'll want everyone to know.

Polly loves his grunting as he thrusts at her, shoves her across the rough chipped desk, his jacket flapping across her thigh, something lumpy in his pocket catching under her hip, the boniness of her buttocks rocking, vertebra rolling in her spine as she arches and sinks, his buttons snagging and flipping on her skin. Beard scraping, rash stinging her chin. She lets her body work, grinding and sliding with him as he moves less smoothly, more jerky, faster, thrusting quickly and desperately, kisses her neck lovely man, his breath rough and loud in her ears.

A taxi rumbles up the street above them. Through the glass bricks in the pavement Polly can see its lights blazing red as it brakes, then all at once her Giles cries out as he comes so hard she's hanging off the table, the blood rushing to her head, making her dizzy, upside down, his cock pushing. Fucking.

And she finds herself fantasising as the sensations pulse through her, imagines Henrietta coming down to find them locked together, horrified but turned on, staying to watch.

This is how it's going to be. She is wild about Giles. He's her man. But he'll go off, fuck Henrietta and other women stretching into the distance. Polly's the lucky one. Even now she can see this is just the beginning. Men, sex, cocks, love, popping corks, for the rest of her life.

Only it's going to get better.

She gasps, how sexy that sounds, and she can't help it. She shudders as the waves break over her, his cock still hard inside her, pinning her to the desk, and the explosion is her coming.

'We have to go,' he says after a quiet moment. He pulls out, climbs reluctantly off her. 'That's Hen's taxi.'

'You just fucked me, Giles.' God, the word 'fuck' feels good in her mouth. The tendons twang as she tries to stand. 'Even though you said I was too young.'

Giles tucks his shirt in. Polly dreads him dismissing her, but he's a gentleman, even if he has just fucked her across his desk.

'Not any more.' He chucks her chin. 'So innocent this afternoon. Such a slut tonight.'

Slut? She was thinking *femme fatale*. 'Just the clothes turned you on? Not me?'

'Yup.' He holds open the door, letting life and light

flood in. 'You'll learn, Polly. Men really are that basic.'

At the bottom of the stairs he pays her. For the waitressing, of course. Though as he hands her £20 extra she wonders for the first time what it would be like to fuck for money.

'So will you take me to the Berkeley Square Ball?' she asks. Upstairs Henrietta is tapping her feet impatiently. Polly smooths her hand over his trousers, strokes the outline of his cock. Well, she's allowed now, isn't she? 'It's not a crush, Giles. I'm in love with you.'

'No you're not, Polly. But you've earned a pay rise.' Pushing her up the stairs in front him, Giles laughs softly. 'And yes, you can go to the ball.'

A Weekend Retreat
by Izzy French

Liz laid her cards on the floor. She'd lost. Again. She was crap at poker. And now there was no going back. They'd all agreed on the rules at the outset. Shivering in anticipation, she awaited Nina's order.

"Time for your forfeit," drawled her friend, obviously delighted that Liz had lost. "Over there and off with your clothes."

She pointed to the corner of the room. Liz could see Joe and Carl throwing back their drinks and looking at Liz expectantly. It was OK for them; they weren't about to get naked. Slowly Liz got to her feet and crossed the room, stepping behind the screen. She was playing for time. And teasing the others a little too, if she was honest.

Liz and Joe had known when they agreed to join their friends for a weekend at a cottage in the country that is was likely there'd be more to it than long, muddy walks and reading in front of the fire. Nina had never hidden the fact that she and Carl were sexually adventurous, and Liz had always enjoyed watching Nina and Joe flirt. It made Joe more attractive to her.

"Perhaps we can share some playtime at the cottage," Nina had suggested to Liz before they came away. Liz had been non-committal in reply. She knew things would change between them if they stepped over any unwritten boundaries. But it was tempting. It was hard not to fancy

Carl. He was a tall, dark and handsome cliché. She'd often allowed herself to fantasize about sex with him. But sex with your best friend's man was something you just didn't do, wasn't it?

The weekend had sizzled with sexual promise from the start. They'd all flirted like mad over dinner on Friday, played 'Truth, dare, promise', all revealing their filthiest fantasies. Their walk in the country on Saturday morning had been wet and playful. Nina had insisted Joe carry her over the worst of the puddles, and Liz had noticed Joe blush and nod when Nina whispered something in his ear. She was obviously plotting. And Liz was happy to let her continue. And now, here they were, on Saturday evening, sated with fine wine and good food, all expecting something more.

The roaring log fire warmed the master bedroom, as they set up their game of poker, pouring cocktails and settling on cushions on the floor. The furnishings were rich. Deep burgundy velvet curtains hung at the windows and a Japanese screen stood in the corner of the room, no doubt to protect the modesty of the lady of the house. Someone suggested they play something like Canasta. To suit their surroundings. But that idea was quickly rejected. No one knew the rules.

"And it's hardly strip poker, now, is it?" added Nina.

They played in silence for some time. The only sound was that of the fire licking and spitting around the logs. Liz could feel a palpable tension between the four friends, she was sure they were all aware of it. It was a pleasurable tension, though. Anticipatory. They were waiting for a catalyst to get the ball rolling. And when she lost the final game, she realised she was the catalyst. It had been inevitable, really. She'd never had a poker face. Unlike Nina, who gave her an encouraging smile as she dismissed her to her fate behind the screen. The warmth of the fire hadn't reached to the corners of the room, and she felt herself shiver with cold and excitement. Behind the screen, there was a small leather stool and a full-length ornate mirror, tilted slightly. Liz could see flames reflected in the glass, and shadows dancing over the ceiling. On the stool lay a black satin blindfold. Nina has thought of everything, smiled Liz, picking it up and turning it over in her hands. Laying it back on the stool for now, she began undressing slowly. The others were murmuring behind her – she didn't dare wonder what they were saying. Once naked, she raised her head to appraise herself in the mirror. Her breasts were firm and high and her nipples hardened as she circled them with her forefingers. Then she ran her hands down her waist and over her full hips and round belly. She liked what she saw and felt. She pressed her right hand over her trimmed pussy hair and reached back for her slit and, caressing her clitoris, watched herself in the mirror.

"Are you ready yet?" Carl's voice called.

She ignored him. She'd bathed earlier with scented oils, anticipating what might happen tonight. Her skin shone, and felt soft to her touch. Increasing the rhythm of her fingers, her pussy tightened and throbbed and her juices ran down her fingers. She pushed her left hand deep inside her cunt. She could come now, quickly, if she wanted to. Just knowing that they were there, on the other side of the screen, waiting for her, was turning her on. It would be quick, easy. She tightened round her fingers. But if she continued now it would be over quickly. The possibility of much more pleasure awaited her on the other side of the screen. She needed to take a chance. To seal her fate. She picked up the blindfold and tied it round her head, finishing with a careful bow, then, feeling her way to the edge of her screen, she stepped out to face her audience.

The blackness was overwhelming. Defensively, she put her hands out in front of her, feeling only air, and took a few steps forward. She could hear low voices and rustling. When she'd left the others, they'd been sitting on cushions on a plush oriental rug in the centre of the room, lit only by the fire and a few candles.

"Wow," Carl's voice exclaimed. "You're beautiful. Joe you are a lucky man."

A hand took hers and led her across the room.

"Sit, please." Nina's voice was firm. Liz sat on one of the high straight-backed chairs she'd noticed earlier. "Time to begin."

Liz remained still. Her body was taut with anticipation. She sat upright in the chair. The flames from the fire flickered, offering her warmth again. Then someone took her hands and tied them behind the back of the chair. Another pair of hands pulled her arse forward slightly and pushed her legs apart, exposing her pussy. She surrendered herself, allowing the hands to position her; quite sure the surrender would be the start of something sweet.

Then someone kissed her. A deep, insinuating kiss. It was Nina. Her full, soft lips tasted sweet. The kiss became increasingly urgent, the tongue twisting around her own, teeth nibbling her lips. Liz's body began to respond and she returned the kiss, her legs parting further as desire throbbed through her. Nina sat on her lap, their pussies touching. Nina's soft thighs were naked too, the rustling sound she'd heard earlier had been clothes being discarded. The kissing continued. Liz wondered what the men were doing. Nina's hands ran swiftly over the curves of Liz's body, stopping to cup her breasts, then ran down her hips and along her thighs. Her touch was smooth but firm. Liz's arousal was increasing, her skin sensitive to the lightest of touches. Her friend's pussy pushed against her own, their pubic hair becoming entwined as they pulsed against one another.

Liz groaned with desire, wishing to touch her friend in return, to grind her fingers into her soft wetness. Nina's hand reached down to Liz's slit and parted her lips, exploring her folds. Liz writhed with excitement. Her friend's touch was delicious. She knew how to please another woman. Her fingers circled Liz's clitoris then pinched it gently, sending shocks of pleasure through her body.

"I want to touch you," groaned Liz, pulling away from the kiss. Her lips felt bruised.

"Keep still," replied Nina. "There's two men here happy to deal with me."

Liz moaned her response, her juices flowing over Nina's fingers and she gave herself up to the moment. Then she felt two mouths on her breasts. Carl and Joe. She pushed her chest forward, wanting them to devour her. She recognised Joe's tongue as it circled her nipple, slowly, sweetly. Carl's mouth was rougher, nibbling, biting, attempting to take her entire breast in his mouth. She felt both men's hardness press into her hips and she pulled against her restraints.

"Time to release her?" Carl asked, acknowledging that Nina was in charge.

"Yes," she answered. "She's ready. It's time for her to please us."

Moments later, Liz's hands were freed. Reaching sideways she found both men's cocks standing erect, ready for her hands to take them. Knowing exactly how to caress Joe to bring him to a long, slow climax; she would do the same with Carl. So she ran her hands down their whole length, cupped their balls and ran her fingers back to the tips, where moist beads of come lay. Then she firmly squeezed and pulled on them both, increasing her speed, feeling their balls tighten, knowing that she was bringing them both close to melting point.

Then Liz gasped as she felt Nina's fingers push inside her. Her pussy pulsed with desire around her friend's fingers as they slid in and out of her. She matched the rhythm on the men's cocks.

"I think it's time to remove her blindfold, boys." Nina instructed.

A deft hand untied the bow behind Liz's head and she shook her hair free. The sight before her only served to increase her desire.

Both men were close to climax. Joe was finger-fucking Nina in return for the pleasure being given to his girlfriend. Nina smiled at her friend as she rode her boyfriend's fingers. Then she pulled away from him.

"Just need to check on your readiness, Liz," she whispered, her voice hoarse. Liz continued to stroke the two men as her friend buried her face in her pussy. Nina licked and sucked her clit, drinking in her friend's juice, circling deep into her cunt. The feeling was exquisite; Liz was close to melting, ready for surrender. Just as the waves of her orgasm threatened to tighten round Nina's tongue, her friend withdrew. She nodded at Carl. Pulling himself from Liz's grasp, he gave himself some quick strokes with his right hand and knelt before her. Nina took his place at her side and began circling her clitoris again. Holding her thighs, Carl began to push inside her. She groaned as he filled her, moving slowly at first, then faster, thrusting into her, fucking her hard.

Nina led her friend's hand to her own dripping pussy,

pushing her fingers deep into her cunt. Liz was happy to be led, seeing from the look of pleasure on Nina's face that her release was close.

Joe was the first to climax, with Liz's expert ministrations. He groaned as he came over her hand and she smiled as she slowly licked the familiar tasting come from her fingers. He rested his head against her breast, taking her nipple between his lips.

Liz turned her full attention to Nina, taking one heavy breast into her mouth as she continued to finger fuck her. She watched as her friend climaxed, feeling the rush of juice and her tightening round her hand. In turn, Liz felt waves of pleasure rush through her, her own pussy tightening around Carl's cock. She looked at Nina's face, twisted now with desire. Her friend's pleasure gave her permission to let go completely and she threw back her head and groaned as her orgasm pulled Carl into her throbbing, tightening pussy, and drew him to his own climax.

A few moments later, they fell to the floor in a tangle of warm, wet limbs, each satisfied, for now. Nina was the first to speak.

"Well, here's to fucking with friends," she raised a glass, then drained it. "More poker, anyone?"

Better Than Chocolate
by Amelia Thornton

God, it had been a long day. Work had been a constant stream of rude, difficult people all deciding today was the day to call up and make incredibly awkward requests, and the new temp had misfiled nearly all of my customer records, resulting in me spending my whole lunch break hunched over the filing cabinet trying to resolve it. The admin girls all seemed to think February 14th was *carte blanche* to do no work whatsoever except giggle over who got which Valentine's card, and if I saw another Interflora moron coming in with a personalised bouquet I swear the whole office was going on lockdown. By the time 5 p.m. rolled around, I was in no mood for enjoying any kind of romance, especially as I still had a huge pile of invoices to go through before I could even think about getting out of the office, not to mention the cloyingly sweet goodbyes of all the girls as they left to head home for boxes of chocolates and rose-petal-strewn beds.

It was nearly 7.30 by the time I finally switched off the lights and headed for the lifts, my head developing an irritating ache and blisters rubbing on my feet. Aaron was no way getting lucky tonight. Part of me felt bad, as he always loved Valentine's Day and all of that kind of thing, but I could just never get myself into the spirit of all that commercial junk. "Just a marketing ploy by the card manufacturers and confectionery industry!" I had grandly informed him on our first Valentine's together. I smiled to myself as I thought about him. Maybe we could still have a nice evening together, even without all that Valentine's junk. Maybe I'd be in the mood by the time I got home.

By the time I'd endured the bus journey back to my place, I wasn't feeling any more inclined, and in fact just more tired and irritable than before. I ran a hot, steaming bath, peeling off the layers of my work clothes and slipping beneath frothy lavender-scented bubbles, and gradually began to unwind a little. I guess some nice underwear could probably do it. That wouldn't be too much effort. I had bought a nice burgundy set back in the sales he'd not had a chance to see yet, and it would at least get me in the right frame of mind. I towelled off my wet body and rubbed my favourite moisturiser into my skin before dressing myself in the new lingerie and a simple black cashmere sweater and short, pleated black skirt. Surely he would appreciate that, at least. I touched up my make-up, grabbed my coat and car keys, and headed over to his.

He opened the door, planted a kiss on my cheek and just wordlessly led me through to the lounge. This wasn't like him, to be so quiet, and I began to puzzle at his mysterious attitude. Had he gone and got me some stupid present, like I asked him not to? Well. What I saw certainly beat a box of Milk Tray, there was no denying that. There it was, right in front of me – just about the finest Valentine's present an anti-Valentine's girl could hope for. Around his tightly muscled torso was a large red ribbon, tied in an elaborate bow at the front, and on his bottom half was nothing but some tight black briefs. Certainly not what I expected to find in the middle of the lounge on a chilly February 14th. I turned to Aaron, grinning stupidly like a kid in a candy shop, and saw that he was beaming just as much as I was.

"Is this really for me?" I asked incredulously.

"Of course. I know Valentine's isn't really your thing, but I thought this might change your mind." He put his arm around me and turned appreciatively to the toned young man in front of us, surveying his lean arms and broad chest with admiration.

"I was kind of hoping you might want to share though," he added wickedly, his eyes still running across the tight muscles of the shoulders, the strongly featured face with welcoming eyes and an even more welcoming smile. I felt a flicker of excitement in my stomach as I thought about Aaron's hands running across this strange new man's skin, their tongues twisting around each other, bodies pushed close together ...

"So where did you find him?" I asked, pulling myself back to the reality of the moment. I was quite aware I was still talking about him like he wasn't there, but it was very hard not to objectify a man standing half naked with a ribbon around him.

"A little bit of internet research, that was all," he replied casually, smiling at the man. "It's amazing what you can find when you put your mind to it ... Dylan, isn't it?"

For the first time, my Valentine's present spoke, sounding almost shy, which just made him seem all the more endearing.

"Er, yeah ... nice to meet you," he said with a sheepish grin. "I hope I made for a good surprise?"

"Well you could say that!" I laughed, stepping closer to him, reaching for the ends of the ribbon, and releasing them with a tug. "I've not had anything quite so enticing to unwrap before, that's for certain ..."

His sharp blue eyes met mine with a teasing glint. "Well, for the next 3 hours, I'm all yours ... so I hope I can do more for you than just get unwrapped?"

I barely had time to cringe at the cheesiness of his line before his soft lips were on mine, pressing gently at first, tentatively almost, until my tongue slipped into his mouth and he began to respond more intensely, biting on my lower lip, his strong hands gripping my hair, a tiny whimper escaping from my mouth as his teeth teasingly clamped down on my tongue. There was something strangely exciting about kissing a man who wasn't Aaron, the different feeling of his mouth, the rush of adrenaline of someone new. Yet this was nothing compared to the knowledge that he was standing right there, watching me, his eyes darting all over my body, drinking in the sight of another man's lips on mine.

I pulled away from Dylan just long enough to glance over at Aaron, his cock straining against his jeans, a wicked grin on his face, his hand gently rubbing the bulging denim, moving nearer and nearer to us. He wanted this as much as I did. With Dylan's lips hungrily caressing my neck, I pulled Aaron towards me, my tongue instantly in his mouth, his kisses just as passionate back. Like a tangled mess of limbs, we fell back on the sofa, Dylan's hands running across the swell of my breasts beneath my tight black sweater, Aaron's caressing the length of my leg, encased in shiny black stockings, gently lifting my skirt to expose the glimpse of pale thigh above them. As he slipped it back down over my legs to reveal my deep burgundy suspender belt and panties, I was suddenly very glad I had bothered to put decent lingerie on after all ...

His fingers inched further up my thigh towards the damp lace of my panties, my breath quickening as his thumb pushed aside the flimsy fabric, moving towards the slick wetness of my opening. Gasping, I felt two fingers pushed roughly inside me, curving around immediately to hit my g-spot as Dylan pulled my legs further apart. Aaron's strong hand thrust deeper inside me, hitting me just right to make me moan each time, as Dylan pulled my sweater above my breasts, revealing the firm curves of my cleavage, framed by deep burgundy lace. My nipples were teased to responsive erectness beneath his fingertips, his tongue wetly fucking my ear as Aaron continued to massage my g-spot, his thumb curling around my throbbing clit and rubbing in a circular rhythm just the way he knew would drive me crazy as his mouth found my other nipple and began to suck.

"God … yeah … don't … stop …" I managed to stammer, as the intensity began to agonisingly build, my whole body alive with sensation as two sets of hands and mouths continued to pleasure me, until finally I felt myself come crashing over the edge, my muscles rippling tightly around Aaron's fingers as orgasm engulfed me.

Panting, I lay there recovering as the familiar glow began to subside, both men grinning at each other like they had just discovered some exciting new trick. Neither even needed to speak as they leaned right across me, hungrily grabbing for each other, their tongues darting inside each other's mouths, two hardened cocks begging for release. Dylan reached for Aaron's flies, frantically tugging the jeans off as Aaron yanked his T-shirt over his head, Dylan's hands deftly pulling Aaron's straining cock from his boxers. I watched, entranced, as this strange young man began to play with my boyfriend's rock-hard cock, his fist tightly gripping the shaft, his free hand caressing his balls. I soon forgot all about my fading orgasm as Aaron slipped Dylan's snug black briefs to the floor, revealing his short, thick cock and tight balls, and dropped to his knees, his lips closing over the throbbing head. Dylan's fingers gripped his hair as Aaron's mouth worked on his cock, saliva running the length of his as he took it deeper and deeper, my eyes never leaving the sight of the mouth that kissed me goodnight sucking cock on the floor of his lounge.

Slowly, I slipped my fingers back inside my soaking panties, my clit still hypersensitive yet longing to be touched. Gently, I began to rub back and forth, keeping with the building rhythm of Aaron's mouth on Dylan's cock, sparks of the beginning of another orgasm darting through me as I quickened the pace of my fingers. Just as I finally began to pay no attention to them, and was closing my eyes, leaning my head back to allow another wave of pleasure to peak inside me, I realised they had both stopped, and Dylan was now standing in front of me, rolling a condom onto his throbbing purple head. Aaron stepped behind me, spreading my legs apart as Dylan pushed inside me, his thick cock widening my tight, wet hole and thrusting roughly into me. My fingers snaked back to my swollen clit, rubbing furiously as he pounded my aching pussy, Aaron's fingers tightly gripping my nipples as I finally came in a shattering jolt. As my muscles clenched even tighter around Dylan, he plunged into me one final time and with a guttural roar came himself.

We both lay, spent and exhausted, sweat clinging to our skin. I glanced over at Aaron, and saw that his cock was still firmly standing to attention, his fingers tightly gripping it and slowly pumping, droplets of precum glistening on the head.

"Come here," I murmured, motioning him next to me, taking him deep into my mouth. Running my tongue along the length of his shaft, I moved aside to allow Dylan next to me, his own tongue hungrily lapping at my boyfriend's cock. The two of us took turns swallowing him, kissing each others' lips over the swollen head of Aaron's cock, my fingers gently probing his balls as we both sucked him. Dylan reached over to his rucksack, lying upturned on the floor next to the sofa, and scrambled around until he pulled out a travel-size bottle of lube, and flicked the lid.

"You wanna fuck me?" he asked, an impish glint in his eye. "You wanna feel your cock pushing on my tight little asshole?"

The eager expression on Aaron's face told him all he needed to know. Bending over on all fours, he offered his tight, tanned butt to the other man. Skilfully, Aaron rolled a condom down the length of his cock, pouring a generous dribble of thick gel over it, and worked a little into Dylan's asshole with his fingers. Spreading my legs in front of him, I pulled Dylan's face towards my already-longing cunt, and sighed with pleasure as his tongue began teasingly flicking against my clit. He grunted deeply as Aaron began to ease the length of his cock into his slick hole, slowly working his way in, Dylan's tongue still darting hungrily between my legs.

I looked up at Aaron, his eyes closed in satisfaction as he made his final thrust and fully entered Dylan's ass. It was so sexy, to watch him begin to slowly fuck the other man, his balls slapping against his toned cheeks, Dylan's own cock already beginning to get hard again. Moaning gently, I pulled Dylan's mouth closer, rocking back and forth as his lips sucked on my swollen clit, my fingers pulling on my own nipples as I felt yet another orgasm gradually escalating inside me. Dylan's panting as Aaron fucked his ass only excited me more.

My whole body bucked forward as my third orgasm ripped through me, my fingers almost pulling out Dylan's hair as I buried his face between my legs. As if spurred on, Aaron plunged ever more frantically inside Dylan's entrance, pounding him until he almost collapsed on top of him as he shot his load. At last, it seemed like all three of us couldn't take any more. We lay, sweaty and panting, in a heap on the floor, at last all completely satisfied.

An hour later, as I curled up on the sofa with a glass of wine, Aaron on one side and Dylan on the other, I couldn't help but think that perhaps Valentine's Day wasn't so bad after all. I mean, it might still be a bit of a marketing swizz, sometimes … but I'll bet those card manufacturers certainly hadn't planned on a Valentine's present anything like mine.

Dr Charm
by J. Manx

I'm a bit of a romantic by nature. I blame this on my mother. Well educated and considered sophisticated, she had a secret vice. She was a Mills and Boon addict. While other women responded to their vices by dieting, exercising and therapy, Mother fed hers with a diet of romance fiction. Once a week, she would take me shopping to a local parade of shops which included a second-hand book store. Mother would never normally take me shopping; she was usually far too busy. However, she allowed me on these local jaunts so that I could help her lug back carrier bags full of pulp fiction. My father would pick up the books and snort with laughter at the improbable names of the heroes: 'The honourable James Salle de Bain, Sheik Rafiq al a Mein, Count Rocco Castellane, and Raphael Montaigne.'

Between the ages of 12 and 14, these books added spice to a dull reading regime of set school texts. The romance and the sexual tension gave me what I thought was a useful insight into the adult world and encouraged my developing sexual awareness.

There were various categories of romance: Wild West, historical, spy thriller, old-fashioned, intrigue, regency, enchanted, the list went on. My favourite of the genre were the 'Medical' series. In these, doctors or surgeons with names like Nathan Dauphin or James Raphael du Perignon, would be the stars of rollercoaster romances. The plots were basic and varied little, but I was amazed at the range of those subtle variations. A brilliant, young surgeon is ignorant of the pretty, conscientious ward nurse. However, when he sees the way she helps his mother recover from an operation for Alzheimer's (using a technique he has developed) he falls in love with her. The handsome but arrogant doctor, who works hard and lives fast, falls in love with the demure practice secretary, when, having been blinded while acting foolishly with a model in his Porsche, is led back to health and learns to appreciate that looks aren't everything. Or, the handsome doctor with the speech impediment who finds it difficult to ask out his stunning, but sensitive, practice midwife who is bored with the attentions of playboy millionaires … Anyway, you get the picture. I eventually cast the books aside in favour of other adolescent pursuits but the stories had left a faint print on my subconscious.

Have you ever heard the expression what the mind expects tends to happen? Years later, when I was twenty-two and during my final year at university, I went, with my closest friend Miranda, to a 'psychic fair' exhibition in London. At the exhibition there was a tarot reader. We went in for a laugh but I came out with a mission.

I had seated myself, a little nervously, in front of a pleasant, middle-aged man who passed me a pack of cards and asked me to shuffle them well. As I did so, he made polite conversation. Where did I live? What did I do? That type of thing. After a while, he told me to stop and I handed back the cards.

'Do you read much?' he asked as he began laying out

the cards.

'Not much, I used to,' I said, raising my eyebrows.

'Why the raised eyebrows?' he said, smiling.

'Oh, I used to read Mills and Boon, not something I'd admit to at university.

The man smiled. 'We all have our vices.' He finished distributing the cards and looked at them solemnly. 'You're unmarried ...' he began.

When I came out of the tent, I was trying to remember everything he'd told me. We discussed what he'd said to each of us but truthfully I wasn't really listening when Miranda told me her future; I was secretly thrilling over mine. Apparently, I was to have a fairly decent job, no major health problems and I would be financially secure. My mother would die of a heart attack in fifteen years time and my father would follow shortly afterwards. But listen to this. I would meet and marry a doctor, have three children and a very happy marriage. Through the doctor, I would find the confidence to develop my own business which would be extremely successful. I'd asked quite a few questions about the doctor. When would I meet him? What would he look like? How would I know he was the one? Apparently, I wouldn't meet him for a few years. He would be about 10-12 years older than me. I would meet him when I least expected it. I remembered the clairvoyant's parting words:

'Just go out and enjoy life, things will happen when they happen. Whatever will be will be.'

So, for a good few years, I did enjoy myself; plenty of boyfriends, plenty of fun but always keeping my eye out for the man in the white coat. I moved several times over the years and each time I registered with a new doctor I wondered whether this would be the one. I attended hospital a few times, once with a friend who'd sprained her ankle, once on my own when I'd fractured a wrist. I took the opportunity to visit a work acquaintance in for a hysterectomy on as many occasions as decorum would allow; each time, hoping to bump into Mr Right.

I was twenty-eight when I eventually gave up hope, realising the stupidity of my superstitions. My mother had warned me.

'You'll throw your life away on the say so of a man who made a bit of money out of you all those years ago. While you're looking out for Mr Right, he may have been there all along.'

Then it happened. I was invited to Miranda's to stay for a weekend. Miranda had married some years ago, divorced and then got married again to a rich accountant. They were loaded. They had an enormous house in the Sussex countryside. She loved entertaining and, I suspect, showing off a little bit. We'd remained firm friends since university and she'd made a number of attempts to pair me up with some of her husband's rich friends. I didn't fancy any of them and none of them were doctors.

I'd arrived at the house early, had lunch, an afternoon nap, showered and dressed myself for the evening. I went downstairs and as I entered the kitchen, Miranda, who was up to her neck in preparing food, looked up. 'Wow, you look gorgeous,' she said, generously.

'You certainly do,' said a voice to my side. I looked around and saw a man sitting at the kitchen table wearing a broad smile. He looked me up and down, quite unselfconsciously and raised his eyebrows. 'I love the shoes,' he said.

I'd put on some new red, four-inch stilettos. I'd spotted them several weeks ago. The ankle straps were beautifully designed and I couldn't resist buying them. It was the first opportunity I'd had to wear them. 'Thank you,' I said, a little unnerved by the man's forthright compliments. He was attractive and there was a mix of humour and lechery in his eyes.

'Oh, I'm sorry,' said Miranda, 'Georgina,' she said, raising her eyebrows at me in a 'pay attention' kind of way, 'this is Dr Luke Daniels. Luke, this is one of my oldest friends, Georgina.'

My heart had missed a beat and I felt myself reddening. Luke got up, took my hand and smiled. The next hour or so, I can't really recall. We drank wine and chatted, the three of us, while Miranda carried on preparing the evening's food. I remember laughing and flirting outrageously. He was really good company and, although about ten years older than me, damned attractive. I knew that he was the one.

'Right,' said Miranda, 'hubby will be back soon and the others will be here in an hour or so, I'm going to have to get ready myself. Miranda, would you be a dear and show Luke where his room is? It's next to yours.'

She gave me a look of encouragement and I could have kissed her.

What a great friend.

'Come on then, Doctor,' I said, seductively, 'let's show you to your room.'

I led the way, mounting the stairs with Luke behind me. I hoped he was watching me. In fact, I knew he was. I consciously stood straighter and added a little swing to my gait. I could feel his eyes on my legs and bottom as I slowly mounted the stairs. Thank God I'd worn the stilettos. If he was half a man, he'd have a raging hard-on seeing my bottom swaying provocatively in front of him. I really laid it on. In fact, I was concentrating so much on arousing him that I wasn't paying attention to where I was going. While climbing several steps separating two landings I slipped and fell over, twisting my ankle. I twisted into a sitting position and began to massage my ankle, a little painful but not as painful as the embarrassment I felt. Luke came to the rescue. He bent down and held my hand.

'You OK?'

I felt a nervous shiver run through me.

'Oh, I'm fine, the ankle's just a little painful.'

'Here,' he said, sweeping me into his arms, 'let's take a proper look at you.'

I directed him through to my room where he laid me on the large double bed.

'Now then,' he said, slipping off his shoes and climbing onto the bed, 'let's take a good look at you.'

I felt as though I was in a romance fiction. I'd waited all these years and here it was happening so quickly I was having difficulty keeping up with it all. Luke knelt in front of me and lifted the foot I had twisted. The pain had subsided and it actually felt OK but I had no intention of telling him that. He examined my foot, gently prodding my ankle here and there.

'Feels OK,' he announced. 'Let's just compare it to the other.' He held both feet together, by the heels, and looked up and down the length of my legs.

'You have beautiful legs.'

'Thank you,' I said, a little surprised.

He lowered one foot onto the bed then held the other and began to caress the 'injured' ankle.

'This should help the circulation, ease the pain a bit, how does that feel?'

'You have a wonderful bedside manner,' I said.

It wasn't just my ankle that Luke was caressing. His hands were running up and down my calf, over my ankle, caressing the heel and toe of my stiletto before his hand returned to my calf.

You randy, old bastard, I thought, happily, pleased by the fact that my future husband was starting appreciatively from the bottom up. I was thoroughly enjoying the attention. I leant back on my elbows as Luke carefully undid my ankle strap and removed the stiletto. I had been meticulous when painting my toes before setting off, conscious that my feet would be on show. They were soft and very pretty. Luke took my foot in both hands, bent down and kissed it.

'Is this a new sort of medical treatment?' I asked, amused and excited, a doctor at my feet.

'This is my treatment for irresistible feet,' he said, caressing my foot. He took each toe in his mouth and sucked and licked it in a most professional and attentive manner before moving to the next toe. It was like having a gentle massage but it was arousing as well as relaxing. By the time he'd moved onto the second foot, I was in a state of lazy arousal.

'Doctor,' I said, 'I think the feelings moved from my ankle all the way up to my pussy. Can you do anything about it?'

He grinned, lasciviously, before moving up beside me, running his hand up my thigh as he did so. Luke kissed me, exploring my mouth and neck, whilst gently massaging my pussy.

'Does this feel better?'

'Oh yes, Doctor,' I said, breathlessly. 'Don't you think you should take out your thermometer and take my temperature?'

He laughed, jumped off the bed and stripped off.

'Good idea,' he said 'you are, after all, one very hot woman'. He had a lovely body and a beautiful cock. God, it had been worth the wait. I leant over, took hold of his cock and pulled him back onto the bed.

'You just put this inside me and I'll show you how hot I really am.'

Luke laughed and pulled off my panties. I spread my legs wide and pointed my toes. He ran his hands up and down my legs and then lowered his head between them. I felt his tongue and mouth and put my hands around his neck and let him enjoy himself. God, he was good, it must have been his medical training. I groaned with pleasure, but after a while, I couldn't bear it any longer. I needed his cock.

'Oh, Doctor, Doctor, I'm an impatient patient, I want you to fuck me, pleeeeease!'

Luke raised himself up and entered me. We fucked, roughly, my legs over his shoulders, hands gripping his buttocks. I came quickly, but the orgasm was intense. We lay afterwards, breathing heavily and holding hands. My prince had come.

After several relaxed minutes, I broke the silence.

'So,' I said, 'how long have you been practising medicine?'

'What do you mean?'

'How long have you been a doctor?'

He looked at me, quizzically and then started laughing.

'You think I'm a medical doctor? I thought you were role-playing … now I see. No, no, no, I'm not a medical doctor, I have a PHD. I'm a Doctor of Philosophy – I'm a sociology lecturer.'

I must have looked stunned because he cracked up

again. He was in fits of laughter. I felt foolish and annoyed, but his laughter was infectious. Suddenly, I saw things with an amazing clarity. 'You must think I'm really stupid.'

'I think you're really attractive,' he said, seriously. 'I think you're beautiful. Here,' he said, pointing to his cock which had now, to use the medical term, become tumescent, 'would you like another bit of my PHD ... my pleasingly hard dick?'

I laughed. As he began kissing my neck, I said, 'So tell me, Doctor, what is your philosophy?'

Luke turned me over, raised my bottom in the air and entered me again. As I moaned with pleasure, he broke into song, rhythmically moving in time to the tune he was singing;

'*Que sera sera* ...Whatever will be will be ...'

Have you ever laughed while being shagged? It's a wonderful feeling.

I married the old goat a year ago; it's been the happiest year of my life.

Shot to the Heart
by Janine Ashbless

'Hold on,' I said suddenly, my attention caught by a window display. 'I've got to buy a Valentine's card.' Grabbing Oliver by the hand I pulled him into the high street card shop.

'Um. Hold on.' Oliver had every right to look bemused. 'Is this for me? Because if it is, you're not supposed to buy it in front of me.'

'Of course not, silly!'

'And if it's for someone else then that goes double. Not to mention … *Who*? And *Why*?'

I grinned at him as I skipped backwards down the aisles of cards, enjoying being the one to tease him for once. I was in a skipping sort of mood. We'd been going out for two months now and I'd persuaded him to take a day off from his computer and come into town with me. We were going to have lunch and go to the museum – his idea – and then go on to the *Cirque Du Soleil* show – my idea – in the evening. And I was crazy-in-love with this stocky tousled-haired man with the sharp eyes and the five-o'clock shadow that started at ten in the morning. Not to mention the beautiful big cock and that incorrigible sexual appetite. I wonder if his parents knew, when they named him Oliver, that he would grow up into a boy who was always Asking For More.

Now he grabbed me, behind a display of teddy bears

all clutching plush scarlet hearts. We were dressed up against the chill outside but even through our winter clothes I could feel a warning hardness pressing into me. 'Who is it?' he growled, nuzzling my ear and making me giggle helplessly. 'Are you being a naughty girl? Am I going to have to put you over my knee?'

I squealed in protest and pushed him away, blushing because I'd been inadvertently loud and I could see other customers glancing in our direction. 'Shush!' I told him, unfairly, even as the blush worked its way right down between my thighs. Was it a serious suggestion, I wondered? I knew he liked to give my bottom the odd smack in passing, just to show his appreciation of a tight pair of jeans or a short skirt riding up, but that was all. Was he the sort of man who was into spanking girls? I'd always thought of that as sort of freaky, but right now the idea of Oliver laying me over his lap and holding me down, able to do anything he liked to my bottom and to the crack between my cheeks and to my exposed pussy, was so naughty and scary and unexpected that it filled me with a giddy excitement.

He knew that. He could see it in my eyes right at that moment; he knew my sex had suddenly grown all hot and puffy and slick. He caught my wrists. 'Who's it for, then?'

Oh, I was so going to disappoint him. 'My mum,' I confessed.

'What? Really?' He let me go.

'I always get Mum a Valentine's card – and she sends me one. And my brothers and sisters. We've always done that in our family. Don't you?'

'We certainly do not.' He grinned, mildly amazed, like I'd just announced that we dressed in top hats and prayed before a picture of Queen Victoria.

'Well I'd have hell to pay if I forgot to send Mum hers.'

'I've always felt Valentines were about the sort of love you don't share with your family.'

I swatted at him. 'Help me pick one.'

He wrinkled his nose. 'I think you can probably manage on your own.'

But he stood over my shoulder as I looked through the racks, pulling faces or making comments until I was weak from giggling and thoroughly exasperated. There were a lot of cards to choose from – sparkly or upholstered, musical or cheeky or childish – but most were unsuitable for what I intended. Eventually I brandished one at him that was blank on the inside and just had a red heart on the cover, bordered with elaborate gold and black inkwork. 'What about this? I like this one.'

'No way!'

'Why not? It's tasteful. I thought you'd like it.'

'It's completely inappropriate.' He jabbed a finger at the picture. 'What do you think that is?'

'Duh … a heart?' I answered sarcastically.

'Does it look like a heart to you?'

'Yes!'

'Come on. You know what a heart looks like.' He held up a clenched fist to signify a knobbly object. 'It's all covered in veins and it's got blood vessels sticking out of the top and it's nothing like the same shape as that.'

Okay, he had a point. 'It's just a symbol, Oliver.'

'Oh yes. But that does not symbolise a heart.'

Smartarse, I thought. 'Then what is it, then?'

He gave a funny, secretive smile. 'You don't know?'

Smarty-smarty-smartarse. He knew everything, or thought he did. But that was one of things I liked about him: he regarded knowledge as a positive thing. Back where I grew up, book-learning was treated like a kind of Tourette's syndrome – only with much less sympathy. Until I met Oliver, who'd been teaching my evening class on *Home Computer for Business and Leisure*, I'd never been out with anyone like him. 'You going to tell me, Mr Clever-clogs?'

Now he had a wicked glint in his eye. 'I could show you.'

I felt like I was taking a piece of bait, and swallowing a big sharp hook with it. 'Go on then,' I dared him.

'Okay. Come on.'

We settled on a card showing a photo of red roses and left the shop.

He took me to Curzon's, which is a big old-fashioned department store of the sort you don't see much about any more: a family-owned business rather than part of a chain, and just a bit run-down. It's the Land that Fashion Forgot. I don't shop there myself; its clientele is mostly the dowdy middle-aged who remember it from their own childhood. Because this was a weekday morning there weren't many customers in and we had the big open-plan floors almost to ourselves. We wandered through the jewellery sections and crockery and perfume. Oliver held my hand and said very little, just smiled slyly. I let him enjoy being mysterious.

Then he led me up the stairs to the fourth floor and into the lingerie department and I was amazed to find that those dull middle-aged women had a real good thing going with their underwear. The department was big – and the stock wasn't all designed to fit anorexic waifs either. All the labels had French or Italian names on. There were basques and corsets and girdles and stockings and bras of every shape and size – bras to make you look big and bras to make you look small, naughty nighties and control garments and suspender belts. I've never seen so much lace all in one place.

'See anything you like?' Oliver asked. 'My treat.'

'You sure?'

'Oh it will be,' he promised, brushing his lips to my ear and biting gently at the lobe. I shivered.

I started to look through the racks of bras, falling instantly in love with the different colours of contrasting lace. A female shop assistant with a face like a wet weekend drifted over in our direction.

'Can I help you at all?'

'We're fine,' said Oliver cheerily. He had the right accent for that kind of place. She looked us over and then retreated to her counter again as a tweedy-looking lady went up to ask for help. I smiled to myself, stroking a longline slip of red satin slashed to the waist, and failing to imagine the tweedy woman wearing anything like this in a hundred years. I had a push-up bra in dark purple with lavender trim in one hand, and another in wild hues of blue and turquoise and pretty appliquéd flowers in the other, when Oliver came over with his own choice of garment.

'I'd like to see you in this as well,' he said softly.

It was a single-piece body made to look like a ruched Victorian corset, with definite hints of burlesque. The chestnut satin of the side panels was overlaid in peach lace and there were plentiful trimmings of black ribbons and suspender straps. I could imagine how I'd look in it and my mouth watered.

'Are you sure, Ol? This stuff is pretty expensive.'

'Valentine's present. You had a look at the knickers yet?' He drew me gently toward those racks and away from the assistant.

'I bet you want me in itty-bitty thongs, don't you?' I

giggled.

'Nope. I don't have a thing for string.' He turned slightly so that his back was to the counter and anyone watching, and lowered his voice to a warm murmur. 'What I like is those ones with the full panel of lace at the front, all sweet and pretty, and then you turn around and at the back they're cut high so that your beautiful round bum cheeks peek out from beneath the lace band, almost bared.' He was starting to sound a little throaty. 'It's like the curtain going up on the stage at the theatre. Oh god, Nikki, that just drives me crazy.'

'Everything drives you crazy,' I countered as he brushed up against me, gentle but very deliberate.

'Everything about you, anyway.' He took my hand – the one not laden with hangers full of frillies – and pressed it reverently to the front of his jeans. He had a semi on already – a hard curve of flesh that surged up against the fabric and against my fingers. He wanted me but bad, I had to admit, and that eagerness was arousing in the most primal way. I licked my lips. I wanted to rub him harder, but a department store wasn't exactly the right place.

'Okay,' I said. 'So something like this …?' I plucked a pair of knickers in stretchy cream lace down from the rack and checked the label to make sure that they were in my size. The gusset narrowed to a ribbon of lace that would fit snugly up the cleft of my bottom; I could already imagine the slight roughness against my most secret flesh. 'And I need some to go with the tops, of course …'

'Here,' he said, handing me four pairs. 'Now head that way. To the changing room.'

'I'm not sure these are the right ones –'

'Ssh! Quickly! While she's busy!'

Trying to look nonchalant we wound our way between the racks to the back corner of the building where the changing rooms were. In a more modern store there would have been some sort of security, but this place was old-fashioned and understaffed. There was just an outer door and, inside, three cubicles. Oliver hurried me into the far cell and shut the door on us before catching me up in a teasing kiss, all tongue and promise. I wriggled my hips, grinding against him. Two can play at teasing. I was pleased to feel him gasp in response and grow harder.

'You're such a horny git,' I complained happily.

'Only because you're so deliciously fuckable,' he countered.

It was a fair cop: I was already well into the tickly, squirmy stage, and just the pressure of his hands and his crotch against me was making me burn. I giggled softly. 'Does this have anything to do with Valentines?' I asked.

'Oh yes.' Releasing me, he looked around the tiny room, barely longer or wider than the span of his arms, and grinned. 'Better and better,' he said to himself, the three mirrored walls obviously meeting his approval. Our reflections postured all around us, mirror reflecting mirror in an unending succession. There was a narrow wooden bench on one side too, and a couple of hooks on the back of the door; nothing else.

I took a moment to hang up the lingerie on the hooks.

'Coat off,' he whispered, laying his own on the bench and sitting on it. I looked down at him, pouting, then wriggled out of my coat in a mock-stripper style to reveal the less-than-sexy layers underneath: a fine grey jersey-cotton top and a red plaid skirt over thick black tights.

'You going to watch me try on my presents?' I asked, though I thought it obvious. But he shook his head. His eyes were intent on some secret, serious purpose.

'Take your skirt off.'

I unzipped and obeyed, half-smiling but starting to catch his mood. I was embarrassed about my woolly tights, which were rather more practical than sensual, but Oliver didn't seem to be put off. He rolled them carefully down my legs, and helped me step out of my boots before tossing the tights aside. I stood before him bare-thighed, the mirrored iterations of my legs arrayed around him.

One lucky point in my favour: out of all the panties I own – from lacy wisps to striped shorts to polka-dotted cotton (and even the stretched grey overwashed ones that every girl has at the back of her drawer for emergency use) – I'd donned this morning a pair in the style he liked best: full cover at the front and even down over the crease of the thigh, but cut high over the cheeks behind. These were plain black and very soft and flimsy, and my cheeks seemed to glow in contrast to their sober hue. My ass is far from skinny, but it was only under Oliver's admiring attentions that I'd come to really appreciate those full, peachy globes. I gave him a twirl to demonstrate my good taste in panties, and in the mirrors my reflections twirled too.

Quickly he caught me and pulled my bottom to his face, kissing first one cheek then the other, just below the delicately scalloped edge of the cloth. I gasped a little as his hand slipped up between my thighs, encouraging me to widen my stance and part them, for which he rewarded me by cupping the mound of my sex. His hot breath and reverent lips and his moist tongue-tip roamed over the curves of my bottom, his other hand stroking up under the line of my panties until I was flustered and breathing hard. His thumb stroked my pussy lips through the silky fabric, working magical changes on and inside me.

'Oliver,' I whispered frantically. If he kept this up I was going to forget all dignity.

'You're wet,' he said, licking the soft skin of my ass. 'Your panties are all wet.'

'Oh God.' I swear I hadn't been until he started on me. Not until the card shop, anyway. Now he knew all about the shameless seep of my pussy.

'D'you want me to show you the Valentine heart?'

'Is it …?' I knew something was going to happen. I could hear the hunger in his voice.

'Get down over my knee,' he said softly.

Oh. I'd never done anything that kinky. I'd certainly never done it in a public place like this. I blushed pink from head to toe and turned to look at him. He sat on that low bench with his thighs spread, his eyes dark and eager, his mouth set in a tense little smile. Is two months enough to know a man? Enough to put yourself face down in his lap in a department store?

Bending forward, he put his mouth to the silky cloth over my clit and kissed it. 'Trust me,' he said as he looked up.

I took a deep breath and lowered myself over his lap. His thighs were strong, but not soft enough to be comfortable – and he immediately lowered one, tipping the top half of my body slightly toward the carpet. Making my bottom my highest point. My sex, used to being hidden away below, felt terrifyingly vulnerable. I opened my mouth in a little noise of unease but he forestalled any words of mine.

'That's right. Relax. Knees together a bit. Beautiful. God, you're beautiful.' His palm cupped the swell of one cheek, soothing me. With the other he pulled at my knickers, drawing the gusset up tighter between my thighs. 'What a beautiful fucking ass you've got.'

His vocabulary always suffered when he got really turned on, and he was hard for it now; I could feel him through his jeans. When I looked in the mirror facing me I could see his rapt expression. I could see my flushed face and my raised bum and his hands; one on the small of my back and one appearing and disappearing as he caressed my bum-cheeks. 'Oliver – Oh!' I gasped as he tickled my clit.

'Now look over your shoulder.'

Squirming, I managed to look into the mirror behind me.

'Can you see it?'

I saw it: the Valentine heart. I watched as Oliver traced its outline with his hand: the two globes of my upthrust ass, wide above and tapering down toward my thighs, to the narrow placket of my pussy that was today sharply outlined in black. My clit was positioned right at the tip of the heart.

'See it?' His hand made the outline once more, finishing at my clit, teasing its fat little bump through the damp cloth.

'Yes!' I sagged back into a more relaxed position, half-closing my eyes.

'This is what that symbol really means,' he murmured, drawing the shape over and over with his caresses. 'This says … *I want you. Be mine.*'

'Oh yes …'

'*I'm yours, now and for ever.*'

His fingertips teased the veiled clench of my darker hole, then swept round to my sex, inexorable. Where he touched me, I lit on fire.

'*I love you.*' He bent to bring his lips near my ear. 'I love you,' he repeated, his voice deep.

I wasn't capable of coherent response to those

growled words. And the next tracing of the shape stopped me thinking at all, as he slid his fingers under the panty-gusset and into the well of my pussy.

'And this: this is where the arrow shaft enters, Nikki.'

His fingers took possession of my hole, spreading me wide, forcing me to choke down indiscreet moans. I didn't need to look any more, or picture in my head the shape he was making. I could feel exactly what was going on: one finger, then two, slipping inside me. His blunt and wicked fingers, tools of an even wickeder mind. I could feel how wet I was. I could *hear* how wet I was – his hand making little kissing noises in my juices as he worked me. And when he stroked that wet down over my clit I started quivering. My legs spasmed, visible witnesses to the electric shocks he was sending right through my body.

'Cupid's bolt. Plunged in deep. Every shot on target. Straight to the heart.'

I could feel the tidal change in me, that surge of reckless need that would drive everything else from my head. If he kept this up I was going to come: on his hand, in a public changing room. My eyes were open but everything in front of them was a blur, nothing real but the touch of his fingers and the aching hunger between my legs.

'Oliver,' I gasped, clawing at the carpet. 'I'm going to …'

'What? Right here?'

'Yes!'

He pulled his hand out and I nearly screamed. His words came in a rush: 'Oh fuck, Nikki. I've got to – I've just got to have –' Without ceremony he hauled me to my feet and pushed me face-on to the wall mirror. I saw his face over my shoulder, drained of everything but intent, as he yanked my sodden panties down from the curve of my bum and jerked furiously at his belt and zip. I felt his hot hard cock slap against my ass-cheek and then stab blindly at the cleft and then, guided by his desperate hand, find its target. All of a sudden, without my having time to think or protest or draw breath, his cock was plunging inside me, more than making up for the loss of his hand. As always it felt frighteningly big those first few moments; the stabs of pain seemed to send up flares inside my head, lighting the darkness. I tilted my bum up, giving him deeper access, pressing on the glass to push back against him. His hands grabbed at my cheeks and my hips, digging in hard as he started to fuck me.

'Oh God,' he groaned: 'Nikki ...'

I could see him. I could see him as he impaled me from behind, and there was an unfamiliar intimacy in that. I could see the flickers of triumph and delight and helpless awestruck need chasing each other in his eyes. He could see my face too, flushed and shocked, my mouth open in tribute to his onslaught, my splayed hands smearing the glass. It wasn't pretty or romantic, that reflection. I hadn't had time to try on any of those lovely bits of lingerie; I was still in my grey top and my breasts were bouncing against the fabric with each jolt of his thrusting cock, while his jeans were sliding down his thighs. And what's romantic about a ferocious, dirty fuck from behind in a cramped cubicle, Oliver gasping hard and slow, my own panting breaths coming fast and wild? What's romantic, for that matter, about his big dick ramming into my wet hole, filling me over and over again with his meat?

Should I have regretted all the pretty romantic stuff? The flowers and the hearts? I was too busy loving this. Loving getting fucked fast and desperate by this man who couldn't keep his hands or his cock off me.

Then came a furious tattoo of knocks on the door. Oliver paused mid-thrust and we looked at each other in the mirror, wide-eyed, our chests heaving.

'Excuse me?' a woman's voice demanded, cold with suspicion. 'Are you all right in there?'

'Yes,' I croaked as Oliver, grinning, pushed my top and my lycra bra up to bare my breasts, tugging on my nipples. Cruel man. Cruel, dirty, wonderful man. 'I'm good, yes,' I babbled as he tucked his other hand round in front of me and gave my clit the touch it craved. 'Yes, oh yes,' I insisted as he began to thrust again. As my body welcomed the renewed assaults of his cock my need ballooned up, almost without warning. It was like a genie released from a bottle: I didn't care any more. I was going to climax. I screamed 'Yes!' over and over again, my face mashed to the glass, as I came and then he followed – shooting over and over again, deep and strong, into the very heart of me.

There was no further interrogation through the door. I doubt we'd have heard it anyway over our own noises.

When we were spent he clenched me in a bear-hug from behind and kissed the sweat from my temple, whispering, 'Be mine, Valentine.' He gallantly led the way from the changing room too, once we'd shuffled back into our clothes, and he carried both our coats.

Out on the shop floor a scattering of people stood staring. Mrs Wet Weekend now looked like a thunderstorm. Mrs Tweed still lingered, looking shocked, pink spots burning on her cheeks. A couple of junior shop assistants had also been called in for backup but were visibly trying to keep straight faces. Oliver favoured them all with a big easy grin. There was no disguising what we'd been up to: we were holding hands, both flushed and tousled and glowing with pleasure.

The senior shop assistant cleared her throat.

'Lovely,' I said with a huge smile, cutting her off, and brandished the hangers full of lingerie. 'I'll take them all.'

Served, on Wheels
by Sue Williams

I'm not going to lie. I didn't need the money. It was all about the power, and there was plenty. I was there to serve the men, to bring their drinks and food; to wear that tiny outfit, and smile, and let them watch. Always, their eyes were on me, their thirsty tongues laid bare, as I glided by in roller boots, oozing sex like honey. I held my tray up high, my breasts pushed up and out – and oh, they'd fall so silent when I passed!

There were rules in the Roller Bar: no groping, no sleaze, no sex. Naturally, I planned to break all three. Of course, I had my reasons. (He'd dumped me for a redhead with big, synthetic tits. You can work the rest out for yourself.) My second week in, I wore stockings beneath my skirt, so when I swept past, the men would glimpse a flash. Some of the bolder ones would slip their hands up and stroke the strap against my thigh. To be honest, it was nasty – most of them were gross – but it put me in control. They wanted me, desired me. They couldn't get enough. They touched my flesh again and again.

But Justin was different. He was tanned and strong. His eyes always glossed me in a drowsy way, as if I was a gorgeous piece of art. His friends were big-boned jokers who loved to cop a feel. The one they called Lee was the worst: when I cleared his plate, he'd slurp his beer and leave the foam on his lips. Then he'd stare down my

127

cleavage like a salivating dog. The others would laugh – all except for Justin. "Guys," he'd say. "Leave it! I'm surprised she even serves us. She's so amazing! *We* should be serving *her*!"

Valentine's Day was hard that year. The boy, who'd torn my heart in two, didn't even call. In the Roller Bar, I let down my hair and spun like an angel on wheels. The mens' hands moved over me, as if my body could cure them. On my way to the bathroom, I met Justin's friend, Lee. He glanced around, and seeing we were alone, shoved me back and ground his hips on mine. I struggled, but he was heavy. I said, "Let me go!" His hand mauled my breasts; he shoved the other up my skirt. "You want it," he groaned. "Don't fight!" I felt him jerk his zipper, felt his wetness on my thigh. His eyes rolled up. His breath was hot with beer. "Yeah, God, you want it …"

"Not from you!" I yelled, kicking his shin. He gasped, jumped back, and I turned to run. But there, in my path, stood Justin. "What's going on?" he asked, gaze searching mine. Hearing nothing from me, he glared across at Lee. "*You*?" he said, striding up. His arm-muscles swelled.

Lee was backing away, fat palms raised. "Slut was up for it, man."

Justin flung a fist at Lee's stomach where it landed with a thump, and the bastard gave a moan and doubled up. "Is that what you get off on?" he cried. "Screwing with people's lives?"

"She … asks for it," gasped Lee. "Look, mate! She's … a whore!"

It was my turn to lock up: a job I loathed. I was scared of being alone – scared of that thug with a grudge. Once the lights were off, I rolled to the door, but jumped to see a man outside. I couldn't see his face. I fell against the wall.

128

The stranger started knocking. I sobbed, then looked again. He was kneeling, with what looked like a flower between his teeth. He splayed a hand against the glass and said, "It's Jush'tin, baby!" I swear, I could have fainted with relief!

I put on the lights and opened the door, and this is what I saw: a shirtless Justin, on his knees: a spaniel with a rose. I laughed, but he stayed serious, pleading with his eyes. His body was exquisite: golden, smooth. "Sh'weet angel! I'll help you forget him!" I rolled in close, so he could see up my skirt, and lifting my roller boot, placed it on his shoulder. His breathing quickened. He glanced up my skirt. I watched him, as lust filled his eyes. He let out the breathiest moan. When his jaw dropped, so did the rose.

"You want me," I said, "don't you?"

And smouldering up with those come-to-bed eyes, he licked down the length of my boot.

I had an urge to skate around and have him sit and watch, as if he'd come to eat and I was serving. He grinned when I told him and his eyes darkened up. He held me round the waist and pulled my hips to his. Our mouths fell together and he kissed me, long and hard. "So?" he said, his breath on my mouth. "Show me to my table."

I switched on the lights. He lounged in his seat, his arms along the length of it, his eyes trained on me. I held my tray high, then took off, gliding round. He watched, lips parted. I could see his tongue. "Angel," he said, gazing at my skirt. I moved my hips to make it flounce.

"You like the way I serve?" I said. He reached and touched my thigh.

"Oh God," he said, rising. "So much!" He climbed onto the table, and sat there as I twirled. Looking right at him, I reached inside my top, unhooked my bra and flung it away. I unpeeled my skirt, and watched him staring at my sex. The striptease took me over. I shed my layers like glitter. I felt so powerful, skating round so bare. My breasts leapt, as the air licked round my thighs. I passed him and he reached for me, but I swerved away. "Think you could take me?" I called, throwing back my hair. He climbed to his feet, mouth all soft. I sent him a smoulder and rolled right up, but I lingered too close, and he grabbed my thong. "Caught you," he said, with a skewed-up smile. He yanked the elastic. His clutch threw my balance. I slammed into him, then gasped against his chest. Our gazes fused. The tray crashed to the floor. His flesh felt warm. He smelled of mint and heat. "Right," he said. "I'll have a portion of you." I laughed, until he pushed me, right hard across the room, the wheels beneath me whirling, as he slammed me to the wall. "God," he gasped. "You feel ..." Then he sank his mouth on mine and tore my shirt right from me and kissed each aching breast. I was gasping from the shock of him, the power of him, his mouth ... "Beautiful," he murmured. I pulled him to my nipples. His mouth – so wet, so perfect! His teeth – so smooth and hard!

He sank to his knees, and kissed me, through my panties. "Roller Girl," he murmured, as he peeled back my lace. And his tongue ... How to explain it? The feeling of him ... oh ... he found the spot so perfectly, that I became a sea – I swear, I'd never been so wet, so grateful, or so crazed. My splayed hand smacked the paintwork. I flung back my head.

I could tell you of each shudder, and each long, unbridled moan; or how he gasped and panted and thrust himself in me. I could tell you what it felt to place my hands upon his chest: his warmth, his muscles, the way he gripped my thigh. But what you really need to know is just how damp I was: my sex was like a tongue that lapped him up. I felt weightless, in his arms, as he slammed again, again, my bones knocking harder, my sighs so loud and long. "Honey, go hard!" I cried. "Oh honey, go hard, don't stop!" And he worked me ceaselessly, his sex so large and deep. God, the way he felt inside me, his muscle and his length, and how my eyes upturned with each exquisite thrust … Our bodies were so wet that the wall grew slick as oil; and at last, he was so fierce – so gloriously firm – that the very floor beneath us seemed to groan.

Afterwards, he left me sitting in his seat, and returned with a pot of honey. "I'm too tired," I said.

"Baby, it's just snack-time!"

We lay together, as he fed me sticky spoonfuls. He licked the back of the spoon, then pressed it to my breast. "So," he said, as I giggled and pushed his hand away. "I hate to bring it up, but this guy …"

I could hardly think about Lee. "I know he's your friend, but …"

He lifted my chin. "I didn't mean Lee," he said. "He's no friend of mine." I blinked at him, unsure. He stroked my hair. "The boy that left you, angel …" I blushed, as he added, "I'm right, aren't I? That's why you're here."

"I don't understand!" I said. "How …?"

"It's obvious. *You*, working *here* …" He reached for my breast, and circled my nipple. "You don't still love him, right?" he said, arching an eyebrow.

I glanced around the Roller Bar, and knew I had the answer. "Tomorrow," I said, "I'll quit this job."

He played with my rollers, grinning and spinning the wheels. "That's great," he said. He tipped a wink. "But don't lose the boots!"

131

Neighbours
by Elizabeth Cage

'Shut up. Just shut up!'

I buried my head in the pillow, trying without success to block out the noise of the party that was in full swing in the house three doors away.

I was fuming. I'd been working all day on the computer, trying to finish a load of reports from work that were due in Monday. OK, so it might sound a bit sad that when most of my mates were out enjoying themselves on a Saturday night, here was I, at home in bed by midnight. Trying to sleep. But it had been a busy month, I'd been travelling most days and now all I wanted to do was relax at home, get a bit of peace and quiet. Fat chance.

I switched on the radio, trying to drown out one source of noise with another. But the boom, boom of the bass speakers was too much for the soothing tones of the Radio 4 announcer. And it was far too hot to shut the windows, which would have helped a bit. But why should I swelter more than I was already on this stifling summer night because some selfish git had decided to have a full-on, very loud party.

'Bastard!' I shouted, leaning out of the window, not caring if anyone saw my exposed breasts as I looked out onto the road below. This was normally a quiet, peaceful little cul de sac. One of the reasons I liked living here. I'd figured out which neighbour it was, the one with the big house right in the far corner. He'd only moved in a couple of weeks before. And from the lights flashing it looked like the party was happening outside in the garden. No wonder the noise could be heard for miles. I just couldn't put up with it. There had to be laws against such things, noise pollution and all that. My head was splitting by now and the aspirin I'd taken earlier didn't seem to have helped. I'd endured this situation for over an hour. I picked up the phone and left a message for the poor sod who was on the noise rota in the council's environmental health department. Twenty minutes later he called back and I let rip about the party.

'Sorry, love, but Saturday is our busiest night and there's only two of us on duty. At this time of year we can't keep up with all the noisy parties. It could be another couple of hours before we make it over to your side of town.'

'And what am I supposed to do in the meantime?' I protested angrily.

'Hope the party runs out of steam. Sorry.'

I slammed the phone down. I wanted to scream. Instead I thumped my pillow. I wasn't going to put up with this any longer. I was going to tell my inconsiderate neighbour to turn it down – or else! 'Right, that's it, you asked for it,' I yelled, as I felt myself rapidly metamorphosing into Basil Fawlty. I pulled my light summer trenchcoat on over my naked body and slipped my feet into a pair of kitten-heeled sandals. Before I shut my front door, I picked up a heavy-duty torch – not only would it help me illuminate the road, it would also serve as a weapon if things got nasty. And the way I felt, I was more than prepared for a fight – in fact I was spoiling for one.

A set of heavy iron gates prevented me from entering

the garden from the back entrance and as I approached I saw a couple by the wall, indulging in a knee trembler. The guy looked up at me sheepishly and smiled.

'Hi, have you come for the party?' he asked breathlessly between thrusts.

'No, I've come to tell your fucking host to turn the fucking noise down or I'll call the police.'

'Hey, chill,' the guy said before letting out a long groan as he shot his load into the girl he had pinned against the wall. He slid out of her and she said irritably, 'You'd better go and get Alex. She seems a bit pissed off.'

When the guy smoothed himself down, I realised that he was wearing a dog collar – the kind that a man of the cloth wears. Either the local clergy are having a jolly little social gathering, or this is a vicars and tarts fancy dress do, I decided. I wondered if there was much likelihood of getting any sense out of anyone.

The vicar returned minutes later. 'Alex is busy but said do come in and help yourself to a drink.' He pulled the gate open and I hesitated, wondering what I was walking in on.

'I don't want a drink. I want some bloody peace and quiet,' I told him.

'Please yourself,' he mumbled, taking a swig from a can of Red Bull.

Cautiously, I stepped into the garden and made my way towards the brightly lit house and the wide open patio doors.

'Fancy a drink?' asked one of the guests, who appeared to be the Pope.

I glared. Inside, I pushed my way purposefully through a variety of tartily attired females sporting fishnets and garters with tight mini-skirts and men wearing black trousers and shirts, with feeble cardboard white collars. What a cop-out for the men these themed parties were, I reflected. Little effort was required, or indeed put in by the males in these situations. Admittedly, there were a few guys in monk's habits and the odd bishop or two. By contrast, most of the women had gone to a lot of trouble, as was evident in the variety of their outfits – ranging from tight, shiny slit skirts, rubber minis and Kylie-style hot pants with long thigh boots. Ample cleavage was on display, and lots of stocking tops. Great for the men. I felt more irritated than ever by the unseen host, who I'd decided was not only an inconsiderate bastard but sexist with it.

'Have you come as a tart?' enquired an alcohol-fuelled male voice. 'Are you wearing a thong under that coat?'

'Fuck off,' I told him curtly, in no mood for wit. The music was thumping and I thought my head would burst.

'Go on, have a drink,' offered a pretty brunette with black hold up stockings and a short leather dress. 'You look as if you could do with one.'

Sighing, I put down my torch and took the glass she offered, which I assumed to be orange juice. After one sip, I realised it had a kick that told me it was mostly vodka. I looked around me. Everyone seemed infuriatingly merry and happy. The air was thick with the current dance hits, cigarette smoke and laughter. Under normal circumstances, I might have enjoyed a party. And it was hard to get annoyed with people who were being nice. However, I was here for a reason and I was determined not to be seduced by the party atmosphere and the hypnotic rhythmic grooves.

'I need to speak to the host,' I insisted, my voice directed at the brunette and anyone else who would listen.

'What? I can't hear you!' she replied, her hips swaying to the music.

'Alex. Do you know where I can find him?' I persisted.

Suddenly a voice behind intoned deeply, 'I understand you're looking for me?'

I turned, ready to unleash my wrath and my mouth dropped open. I was confronted with a dark-haired guy at least six feet tall, clean shaven with penetrating blue eyes. He was wearing four-inch spiky heels, black, lace-topped stockings and suspenders and the most beautifully crafted Victorian corset in pale blue silk. His mouth was a gash of deep scarlet, his eyes heavily kohled. A snake tattoo encircled his right arm and a rose adorned his left shoulder. His upper torso was toned and muscular. I was instantly reminded of Tim Curry in The Rocky Horror Picture Show, who I've always had a thing about. Specifically dressed like that. I felt myself melting. Quickly, I attempted to regain my composure.

'This party can be heard from miles away,' I pointed out sternly.

'Really? That's good, then,' he replied, grinning annoyingly. 'So you decided to gatecrash?'

'No, and it isn't a laughing matter,' I replied tersely, trying not to wonder what it would feel like to be fucked by such a vision of sensuality.

'Hey, you live down the road, don't you? I've seen you driving around. Nice car. Good choice. Racy.'

'I'm not here to discuss your automobile preferences,' I responded, trying to sound dignified and businesslike.

'Well, why are you here?' he asked, and I realised his eyes were scanning my figure, assessing the outline of my breasts, caressing my knees, my shins, my ankles, lingering on my painted toes. 'Nice feet,' he muttered appreciatively. 'Like the shoes.'

'Forget the feet. I want you to turn down the music.'

'Why? It's great music. Wanna dance?' and he offered me his hand.

'It's loud music. Too loud. I was trying to get some sleep.'

'But the night is young. And it is Saturday. Party time.'

'Not for me.' I sighed. This was going nowhere.

'It could be. You're welcome to stay. It's really hot in here.' He gave a teasing grin. 'Shall I take your coat?'

'That won't be necessary, as I don't intend to stay,' I insisted, blushing. Did he realise I was naked beneath my coat? 'You're not listening, are you? Turn the bloody music down. Please.'

He considered for a moment then said, 'OK. On one condition.'

I groaned. 'I'm not in the mood for this.'

'One tiny condition,' he repeated, moving closer. I could smell his aftershave. Unfortunately one of my favourites.

'I don't like playing games.'

'It isn't a game.'

'So what do I have to do to get you to turn the music down?'

'Kiss me.'

I froze. 'What?'

'Kiss me. Then I promise you I'll give in to your request, however unreasonable.'

'Unreasonable! This is pathetic.' I began to walk away.

'Your call,' he said. 'I reckon it will be ages before the council send someone out to tell me off and the police are far too busy dealing with drunks and fights in town to come all the way out here. Like I said, your call.'

I glared at him. 'Fuck you.'

'Well that would be even better.'

I wanted to slap him. But, more than that, I wanted to leave with my mission accomplished.

'Kiss me,' he whispered. 'Or do you think I'm so repulsive?'

'Quite the opposite,' I admitted. 'But a pain in the arse, nevertheless.'

'So what's it to be?'

I weighed up my options. 'One kiss?'

He nodded. 'Just one.'

'Then you promise to turn it down?'

'I promise. You have my word.'

I grunted dubiously. 'Yeah. Well, you'd better not mess me about.'

I stepped towards him, trembling with a mixture of anticipation and annoyance, which he sensed.

'What are you afraid of?'

'Nothing,' I snapped, leaning over and grazing my lips against his, ready to pull away immediately. But as our lips made contact, his arms enclosed the small of my back, holding me close. As I breathed in the heady notes of his aftershave, I realised my mouth had parted slightly, and, before I knew it, his tongue began to trace a delicate outline of my mouth. I felt my own vodka-infused breath mingle with the wine on his, as our tongues instinctively began a journey of exploration. This wasn't meant to happen. Still, I might as well enjoy the price I had to pay for a bit of peace and quiet, I decided, as I felt my body relax.

I could feel his hands move down my back, over the curves of my thighs through the fabric of my coat. I allowed my hands to rest on, then grip, his broad shoulders and I felt the hardness in his groin pressing against me. All the while, we continued to kiss, drinking in each other's scents, and his fingers found their way beneath my coat, travelling slowly, teasingly. I moaned inside his mouth as first one, then, two fingertips gently brushed the inside of my thighs. In response, he rested his thumb against my rapidly swelling clitoris, exerting a light pressure while his forefingers stroked and probed the spreading wetness between my now open legs. I guessed he intended to make me come and I was more than happy to go along with it, all logic and willpower completely overtaken by lust and sensation. Delicious sensation. I half wondered if we had spectators, but as he continued his rhythmic strumming, which was inexorably building to a crescendo to precipitate my own, I no longer cared who was watching. I felt the tension mounting as my muscles began to involuntarily contract, and as the first wave engulfed me, his mouth was still over mine, our tongues entwined. I felt my groans vibrating in my throat, my chest, my whole body and as the second wave built up, he grabbed my hand and placed it over his hot, rigid cock. I rubbed my hand up and down in rhythm with the fingers that still played my clit, his glistening precum acting as lubricant. As our mutual speeds increased, I felt his body shudder as a jet of come spurted forth, the spray hitting my face and his. When his groans had subsided, he unfastened his mouth from mine and we both gasped for breath.

'Some kiss,' I murmured, hardly aware of the music still thumping and pounding in the background.

He smiled. 'Just being neighbourly. Now, are you sure you don't want me to take your coat?'

Dirty Boy
by Charlotte Stein

He shifts uncomfortably on the seat beside me, but I know what he really wants. He wants me to press closer, the way the couple opposite us in this crowded train carriage are pressing closer, giggling over the goofy Valentine's Day presents they've bought each other. He wants me to put a hand on his thigh – far higher than the girl is doing to her guy.

It's just that he doesn't know that he wants this. They never do. They fumble and fawn and wait for me to make a move that frightens them, but everything always ends up the same: mindless pleasure, delicious right down to the core.

He flinches, when I slide my hand over the sinewy round of his corduroy-clad thigh. The heavy muscle there tenses, twitches – I can feel him looking at the side of my face. I know what that look means: people who put their hands on other people's thighs have to be looking at you. They can't be so impassive, so cool and collected, as to keep staring straight ahead as though nothing's happening.

I'm happy to prove him wrong. I'm sure he's got all sorts of lovely conventional ideas in his silly little head that need turning upside down. Like how much massaging of someone's thigh is permitted, on a crowded train.

'Um ...' he says, but that's all he can manage. The

girl giggles – I think she's seen – but then he unfolds his newspaper over his lap and her view is shut off. I think he does it well enough to make her think there wasn't anything worth seeing, anyway, but maybe it's just that she assumes boring, when she looks at him.

Maybe she just prefers nibbling her boyfriend's ear to caring about needy strangers on a train.

Personally, I think the paper over his lap was a mistake. It's saved him from prying eyes, but it's also given me even more free rein. Of course, I would have jerked him off with my hand inside his trousers in full view of giggler over there, but he doesn't need to know that. It likely soothes him to think that I'm only doing this because we're hidden from view.

And I don't mind, if he needs that small concession. I'm not going to give him any quarter on anything else, after all. I barely wait another second, before I clamp my hand down tight on that crease, between his thigh and his groin.

He hasn't got his legs closed enough, so I'm able to get right down in there. I can feel the subtle press of his balls against the back of my fingers, through the thick material of his trousers – that's how in there I can get. And when I nudge against that soft rounded shape, he jerks back against the seat, hard.

I think he almost stands up. He does this weird little jolt and then his butt leaves the plush two-tone bench we're sitting on, but he doesn't quite make it to standing. The whole move kind of gives the impression that his trousers were bunching in the crack of his arse, and he had to almost get up to relieve the pressure.

He's definitely gone about pressure-relieving in the wrong way. Why, he's barely moved enough to escape the press of my fingers against his tender parts – never mind anything else. And if I just sli-i-ide my hand ever so slightly upwards, I can get at far more interesting things.

It fills me with joy, to feel his entire body moving up with the push of my hand. It's not like he's trying to get away, at all – because Lord knows, going up is not going to achieve that – but as though I'm the puppeteer, and he's my puppet. It's as though he's expressing surprise through extreme body language, the surge-up of his thighs trying to emulate what his eyebrows would usually take on.

The illusion is somewhat shattered when he crams himself right back down into the seat, and urges himself against my hand – though I don't think he intends to. I think he's kind of torn between propriety and perversion, and oh goody I get to see which is the better fighter.

At the moment, perversion is definitely winning. He's breathing hard and crumpling the newspaper into sweaty fists, and when I give the thick press of his erection a little teasing caress, through the corduroy, he slouches very obviously forward.

Of course this makes the jut of his cock press deeper into my rubbing palm, but oh, so sorry. Now that I've caught you I'm bored. I guess you're going to have to work for it, too bad. Maybe you should have been more enthusiastic from the start and I wouldn't have to be such a bitch now, but them's the breaks.

I move my hand back down to the far duller climes of his thigh, and he keens like an underfed puppy. He doesn't need to know that such a sound thrums against my already agitated clit, or that the sudden sharp smell of his sweat in the air makes a slick of liquid flood my slit, or that when I allow myself a turn of the head and see his teeth biting into his lip, warmth radiates through my belly, tightening my nipples as it goes.

There is nothing so sweet as the sight of a man, biting his lip in tortured ecstasy.

I reward him, with a firm stroke against the heavy outline of his cock. He gives back in kind by bucking his hips – just a little, not enough to make the paper crackle and crash about – and letting out a gust of breath that's almost a sigh.

We get a lovely rhythm going. A circuit, I suppose – one thing feeding another. I rub and he stifles a groan or rocks his hips or licks the perspiration from his upper lip, and then I am compelled to rub again. Of course, I'm making it sound as though this happens really slowly, when that's not the case at all.

By the time the elderly woman sitting on his right gets off the train, I have my hand inside his trousers.

It's an awkward angle, but I think I use the heel of my palm to good effect. I rub it nice and tight over the straining underside of his cock – right where it curves up into that neat little ridge. The rest of him is lost to me, the tip smothered by underwear somewhere beyond my grasp, but I think rubbing him like this is doing its job just fine.

He actually whispers a little *please don't stop*, when I make to tease him again. I think he's pretty close to coming all over my hand. Certainly everything feels sticky already, and his thighs are tensing and releasing in an almost hypnotic pattern.

But I don't want him to get there just yet. The girl and her boyfriend aren't paying the slightest bit of attention, and I think that's because he hasn't quite been loud enough, so far. His whispers sound like controversial comments on the day's news. His sighs are almost like exasperation.

I want to put his cock in my mouth.

There are a lot of things I want, but I think I'm going

to start with this, first. I lean to one side, just ever so gently, and whisper in his ear: stand up.

I mean, he was so eager to, earlier on. Why shouldn't he be, now? Putting aside the fact that there's a stiff cock tenting the material of his trousers and underwear, of course. The first eye contact I make with him since this began is when he widens those baby blues at me, fluttering all over with panic and that perfect state he's found himself in – the one where he can no longer just say no.

Still, he hesitates. He chews and chews on that plump lower lip, as I peel the layers of newspaper away. I think after he's obeyed me, I'll make him turn around like someone modelling this season's collection of stylish looks. I call this one: man with gigantic erection.

I let him fumble his zipper back up, but don't concede anything else. When he stands and leaves behind the safety of the crumpled paper, it's without his hands over himself or his body curled coyly to one side. The tent in his trousers stands out obscenely, and the girl across the carriage stifles a giggle into her hands.

I think I feel his flare of humiliation go through me, too. I squirm on my seat, and squeeze my impatient thighs together. Tingles wriggle through me when I ask him:

'Need the bathroom?'

As he stumbles towards the safety of the carriage door. Though it's debatable whether it's safety, when him turning gives everyone a lovely profile view of his solid prick.

I do wonder if he's going to come back. He could very easily hide out in the toilet until the journey is over – and maybe face the music then, when there's no-one else around. But I have faith in him and only a few minutes later that faith is justified.

He returns, still blushing. Tugging at his M&S jumper and wiping his still damp hands on his cords. The damp hands that have probably been washed just to get the tang of spunk off them.

Dirty boy.

Did he really think he could have me miss such a thing, and get away with it? Now I've missed all the lovely detail: him licking a filthy wet stripe over his palm before sliding it nice and slick down the length of his shaft. Doing it nice and hard because he can't wait and knows he only has a few minutes in which he can be disobedient. Thighs trembling, cock swelling tight against his unsteady grip – and then an orgasm that makes his arse cheeks clench and his teeth draw blood.

The thought almost makes me want to go to the men's and check the sink for stripes of come. I want to lick what he's dirtied.

I settle for taking his hand all cute and loving and raising it to my mouth as though to kiss. And then I lick his longest finger from knuckle to tip.

It's only when I get said finger right into my mouth, however, that I taste what he's done. I suck hard, and that musky-salt flavour floods my mouth. It's easy to detect, even under the cheap train bathroom soap. I'm used to boys being dirty, all over their hands and bellies and maybe over me, too.

He clears his throat as I continue licking and sucking his fingers in a manner that the girl and guy across the train seem to think is pretty lewd. When he clears it again, though, that's when I get the picture. Now he's all relaxed he can be disapproving. He can make a little sound that says: give me my hand back.

But then I look at him and a fierce blush swamps his face. Once my eyes are on him, he has to come to terms with the fact that he's just masturbated in a train bathroom and now I'm tasting the evidence on his lovely long fingers.

He doesn't clear his throat again. His eyes go down, and thickly lashed lids drop over them. I bite, lightly, on the meatiest part of his forefinger, and those lids flutter prettily.

He's going to love what I have in store, next. I lean forward, and press my mouth to his.

His lips are parted, so it's not hard to achieve my objective. I just push forcefully against him until his head hits against the seat back and my tongue is pressing wetly into his mouth, and then – oh look at that. He gets to taste what I've just tasted.

I'm generous, that way.

He groans in this meek, almost-disgusted sort of fashion, but he's a fool if he thinks I'm buying it. It doesn't take him long to eat my face off, after all. He's soon kissing back at me sloppily, the hand in mine squeezing and squeezing. His other hand daring to go to my waist. The taste of his come between us, filthy and lovely all at the same time.

When I break away from him, he puffs soft words against my lips: *I didn't mean to*. Of course I could tell him here that I forgive him, that him saying words like that makes me wet, so wet, but that's just not the point of this game. He doesn't need to be soothed and I'm not going to tell him how aroused I am.

Instead, I order him to describe what he's just done in the bathroom.

It's a calculated move. The couple opposite us have gotten bored or embarrassed and both are listening to their Ipods – most likely special sweetheart love song playlists they've both made for each other – so it's safe for him to

146

talk. But it's also still nasty. Good boys don't talk about jerking off on trains.

It's all about balance, I feel.

'Don't make me,' he says, but I don't have to make him. I don't have to say another word – I just stare into his big bright eyes and wait, and wait. Eventually he cracks and whispers, and each sound he makes streams hot air against my lips. It's a sensation I've not really thought about before, but Lord I'm thinking about it now. It goes directly to my cunt, and makes me want to kiss him again, long and wet.

'I went to the bathroom,' he begins, and I silently applaud his thoroughness.

'And then what?'

'Then I … unzipped my trousers.'

He gives a little shrug, as though that's all there was to it. As though he just pissed, then, and came back here. So I stick out my tongue, and flick it over his swollen lips.

Before he continues, he licks my taste off himself.

'My hands were shaking …' he says, as though turning such a detail over and over in his mind. Why on earth had his hands been shaking? '… but I didn't want to stop.'

'I'll bet you didn't,' I say, against his mouth. We're almost kissing, but not quite.

'I wanted to touch myself.'

'I know. I know. Go on.'

'It felt so good to wrap my hand around my co – myself.'

I shiver, to hear him dodging the word *cock*.

'Did you do it hard, or soft? Fast, or slow?'

'Really quick. I jerked myself so hard it kind of hurt.'

'But you liked that, right? That little edge of pain?'

His eyes roll back in his head. I think he's searching

for inspiration. That, or help.

'… yes.'

'You're getting hard again, just thinking about it.'

'I'm getting hard because you're making me talk like this.'

'Is that what I'm doing? Making you?'

'Ye-e-es,' he whines, suddenly twenty years younger than he most likely is.

'Are you sure? If I stop, and pull away, will your erection fade?'

I put my hand over the renewed jut in his trousers, for emphasis. He swallows hard, and looks away at nothing. It looks to me like his answer tastes bitter, but I bet it's sweet, too.

'No.'

'You're going to masturbate forever, thinking of this – aren't you?'

He nods, after the barest of hesitations. His cock jerks, beneath my pressing hand. I almost think he's going to be relieved, when the couple get up at the next station and leave in a cloud of giggles, but the groan that comes out of him doesn't sounds relieved at all.

I think he believed they were his lifeline, tethering him to no-sex-on-a-train. He's wrong, of course, but I'll let him cling to the idea.

When the door closes behind them, I straddle him. He flusters and blusters and says something that might be *oh no wait*. But then my stretched taut and too-damp knickers brush over his equally covered cock, and I think he forgets what he was asking me to wait for. His hips hump up at me – against his will, I'm sure – and he groans loudly, now. The warmth alone must feel good, and it's going to feel even better when I get my knickers down.

Not that I have to. He goes for them suddenly, shoving up under my skirt to yank them down as far as they'll go. They stretch over his thighs like a band caging him in.

'What are you going to do now, hotshot?' I say, and that drains some of the sudden daring out of him. But the heated eagerness remains, and that's what I need the most. As long as that stays, I don't care what else goes.

'I …' he says, so I take back the reins. I always take back the reins. I reach between our bodies and unzip his trousers, take out his heavy-once-again prick.

I bet he's going to come as easily as he did not ten minutes ago, and the thought makes me sigh. My clit swells – my entire pussy swells. I think I'm going to come pretty easily, too.

'Oh – your hand feels so good,' he says, though I'm barely doing anything at all. I just squeeze, lightly, relishing the stickiness and his sharp scent. He washed his hands, but he didn't get any of the mess here.

'Be quick – before anyone else gets on and comes in here,' he demands, but that just shows me how little he's learnt.

'Be quick at what?' I ask, and then loosen my grip on his swelling prick.

'On … uh …' he starts, but of course can't finish. What is he going to say? On the handjob you're going to give me? Jerk me off, now?

How dull.

Instead, I lean in close, and manoeuvre the head of his cock to my sopping slit. I arch my back so that it fits, and then he's right up against my clit, right there – God yes.

'Ohhhh you're all slippery,' he tells me, as though I don't already know.

I forgive him, however, because I'm now rubbing his

149

nicely thick cock against my aching bud, and it feels too good to split hairs. Pleasure radiates outward from the place where we're meeting, and I use his cock like a finger, like a sex toy, sliding it around and around my clit until I'm moaning.

'Are you going to come?' he asks me. 'Are you going to come?'

But I don't get a chance to answer. He tells me how he can't last and asks me to stop, first. *Stop*, he says. *Stop*, as I tug harder on his swelling cock and rub myself all over him. When I feel him spurt against me – that's when I give it up. When his spunk drowns my clit and he pants and bucks his hips up and the train … the train is coming to a stop, again. That's when my body tightens all over and I cry out – loud enough for the whole train to hear.

Bliss.

I allow myself one small sag against him. Just to recuperate. Just to feel him shuddering against me while I come down too. I put my hand to my lips, and taste him one final time.

And then it's back to being me.

I peel myself off him and stand, putting knickers back into place – around a delightful mingling of fluids that I'll be sure to explore later – and my skirt to my knees once more. I watch him do the same – trousers fastened, hair smoothed back – before I sit back down beside him.

He's still breathing hard, when I do. And I think: God, what a wonderful Valentine's Day gift I've given him. Anyone would be thrilled with a present like that and he'll be doubly so because he's like that. There's nothing he loves more than being humiliated and used, I know – I always know – and I'm sure right now he's thinking up something equally as delicious for me. Something that's not chocolates and flowers. Something that's decadently dirty.

Or he would be thinking those things up. I'm sure he *would*. If he were my boyfriend, and not a total stranger.

Tongue Craft
by Alcamia

It was one of those sultry, golden evenings which only the south of France can produce, and I was sitting at the bar enjoying a drink, while the barman, Henri, polished glasses. I had been watching Marius for a couple of hours. He was built like a bull, large and rugged, his skin tanned to a deep bronze hue from his work down at the docks. He had an irresistibly sexual aura, so much so, I couldn't resist being just a little provocative – hitching up my skirt to show him my curvaceous thighs and leaning forward to display the swell of my breasts. Grinning at me, Marius raised his glass and, winking at me, he would show me the tip of his agile, fluttering tongue, before he turned his attention back to the swarm of women who were now clustering around him, touching and flirting with him and making a great fuss of trying to sit on his lap.

'That man over there ... Who is he?' I asked.

Henri leant conspiratorially across the counter. 'You want to watch that one, that's Marius or as he's known in these parts. Langue de chat?'

'Why do they call him cat tongue?' Sipping my drink, I enviously watched as Marius began fondling a pretty blonde.'

'No one really knows how he came by the name, but apparently if you have carnal knowledge of Marius, you know.' A sly smile spread across Henri's face. 'It's rumoured Marius has a most unusual method of seduction. They say once a woman has sexually known him, she is ruined for ever and once licked by Langue de chat, no man will ever be able to satisfy her again. You need to watch his party game to know what I mean. Today's Friday and Marius always plays on a Friday. Soon everyone here will begin to place their bets and the punters will ask him to perform some ludicrous feat of dexterity with his disgusting tongue. To my knowledge, he's never lost a bet.'

Fascinated, I ordered another Daiquiri. I was determined to watch cat tongue's game and discover what made this sexy bear of a man so mysterious.

Marius drank a couple of glasses of scotch and suddenly a plump local woman with fiery red hair and stunning breasts stood up and, fixing Marius with a coquettish smile, she shouted, 'Langue de chat, it's about time you showed us a little of your tongue craft. Whip the monster out and demonstrate what you can do with it.'

The crowd clapped and whistled and Marius, after making a great act of pretending he didn't know what the girl was on about, instantly thrust out his fleshy tongue. It was unbelievable, since I had never seen an oral muscle of such incredible dimensions and flexibility. It was much longer than any tongue I had ever seen before and it seemed he could do amazing and rather obscene things with it. Marius could bend it this way and that and make shapes with it – in fact the tongue could execute such formidable feats of gymnastics, I think it had a mind all of its own.

The pretty redhead, wiggling her hips invitingly, came and sat on Marius's lap and, producing a tape measure out of her pocket, she proceeded to goad him with it. I watched, mesmerised, as Marius teased her back, first of all sticking out his tongue just a little bit and next wriggling it about. However, before she could trap it with her nimble hands, he'd pop it back into his cavern and she would giggle in consternation as her fingers missed the slippery trickster, pressing his mouth instead. Marius trapped her finger with his fleshy full lip and sucked it inside his mouth, all the while whispering in her ear and making her blush as she cried. 'Marius, don't be a tease.'

Soon the small crowd of people around the bar were chanting. 'Get it out again, Langue de chat, get it out.' The erotic fervour of the audience reminded me of the time I'd attended a striptease. The same sexual tension permeated the air and I think every woman in the room was aroused. As the crowd chanted, Marius kept laughing and jiggling the woman on his knees so her large breasts bounced. I'm sure her nimble hand was fondling his crotch.

'Yes, I will get it out.' He said playing to the crowd. 'But only if Angelina the virgin lets me kiss her.'

Stroking her abundant red hair out of the way and pushing her bosoms against Marius's open shirt, Angelina proceeded to part her lips and closed her eyes ready for the invasion. At that precise moment, the crowd held their collective breath and the curious sexual atmosphere intensified. It was as if I were witnessing a rape with the tongue or a mysterious and deliberate seduction. Marius pressed his lips to hers, angled her head with his hand to maximum advantage and began to kiss her, while the woman's body behaved very curiously, giving little orgasmic jerks and twitches. I was aware something unusual was going on and I was not immune to the highly arousing throb of subliminal sex, but it was difficult to tell quite exactly what was occurring within the mouth of the redhead. I began to shift on my bar stool as fierce stabs of sexual longing intensified and I realised my flimsy silk panties were drenched in juices. I couldn't help wondering what it would feel like to have the mysterious Langue de chat kissing me and thrusting his dextrous oral appendage into every one of my bodily apertures.

Needless to say, the kiss lasted a long time and when eventually their lips broke apart, Angelina's face had assumed a drugged expression. She was now pale and breathless and two high spots of colour marked her cheekbones. Marius fixed her with his dark gaze, licked his lips and slowly he pushed out his tongue to its fullest extremity. The woman, now tamed and docile, measured it thoughtfully and nodding her head and pocketing the tape measure, she slid shakily off Marius's knee and collapsed in the arms of her friend, gasping. 'It's amazing, incredible. It's even larger than a dick. I've been savaged.' And then she smiled.

The bar had become extremely quiet.

'There you are. Another woman has been raped by the tongue and now she won't be the same again. It is like witchcraft. She has been tasted by Langue de chat and she will never find satisfaction with another man. She is bewitched by the tongue,' Henri said, shaking his head sadly.

Something about the nature of the tongue aroused me. If you have never seen an appendage like Marius's, you will not know what I mean, but I can tell you a man's penis soon loses it's attraction when you are confronted with a dexterous muscle as long as a ruler, with the ability to gyrate, dart and probe into your most sensual places with the nimble flexibility of an acrobat.

One day, Marius slipped into a chair at my table. 'Do you enjoy my little show?' he asked, winking at me, and stretching out the tongue. 'People freak out sometimes.

However, once they see my performance, they're seduced.' Turning his glass around and around in his fingers, he fixed me with a licentious stare. 'I've noticed you here before, you come alone and you don't have a boyfriend. It's a waste for such a beautiful woman to be on her own. How about I ask you out? There's this nice place down on the beach which has prawns to die for.'

Laughing, I shook back my long brunette hair. 'Oh, I don't think so.'

Spreading his hands in supplication, Marius affected a pout with his provocative lips. 'Why ever not? Ah I know why it is! My behaviour puts you off. You have watched me and you think I am a whore of the tongue and I am prostituting my body. You think to yourself, I don't want to know that randy Frenchman, he's a sleaze. Well I can assure you, my sweet, it's just a party piece and simply for amusement, that's all. At one time, I got a gig in a small and curious theatre where they liked to make fun of people with bodily appendages which were rather out of the ordinary. After a while though, I got bored with it, since there's not much fun in prostituting your body night after night. This is different, I do this purely for amusement. I like to confound women and arouse them. But, I know what you're thinking and, in a manner, it's true. My tongue is indeed like a whore, it finds its way here and there and it does rather naughty things, but ...' Leaning closer to me I felt his breath tickle my neck and my nipples hardened alarmingly. 'Let me tell you, it very seldom gets cunt. I mean, I don't fuck every woman I meet, in fact I'm very choosy. Naturally, girls will spin stories that they've had me, but that's because they're crazy they never got fucked by the tongue of Langue de chat.'

I couldn't resist him. Langue de chat kept flirting and

from time to time his hand would touch my fingers or brush my breasts. I was tingling from head to toe, alight with pulsing erotic thoughts of tongues and penises penetrating me in every secret place. You see, no man had been able to satisfy me in years. I require infinite variety and painfully long periods of foreplay to make me orgasm and my boyfriends soon tire of me easily when their fingers and tongues begin to ache and I fail to come on demand. Now once again I was coming alive like a glowing ember of sex – to delicious erotic reawakening. Marius ignited feelings in me I'd forgotten and many more besides. I could feel my skin thrilling and trembling with the anticipation of Langue de chat's unique tool and the filthy performance it could stage on my feverish body.

'I promise,' he said, pressing his hand to his heart and laughing, 'if you come out with me, I will keep the freak well and truly incarcerated in his hot, little prison cell, and I'll only let it out to play if you ask me nicely.' Then, quickly, he gave me a delicious little kiss on the corner of my lips. How could I resist?

Early on in life, Marius discovered his muscular oral appendage was the key to fame, fortune and sexual fulfilment. Naturally, the tongue was a useful pulling tool, and after a woman recovered from the shock of seeing the long, lean, oral fucking machine flickering away at her – she easily fell for him. Many mysterious tales circulated about the oral gymnast and Marius was fond of recounting stories about the extensive range of kinky oral acrobatics his chunky muscle could perform.

'You know,' he said, 'it's curious how I became the local celebrity because at school I was quite a freak. Kids are so observant and they immediately pick up on you if you are different.' Crossing his long legs, he fixed me with an impertinent stare. 'Whenever I was sitting eating

157

my lunch, the other kids would all be staring at me, waiting to catch a glimpse of my tongue and it irritated me so much I couldn't help poking it out and showing it to them. Other little boys liked flashing their penises, I enjoyed flashing the tongue. I'd artfully knot it up and flex it, just to make their eyes boggle, until, as fate would have it, the local bully Pierre, caught me out the back, by the toilet block. He was head of a gang and they picked on any kid who was a bit different. Well before I knew it, they'd tied me up and made me get on my hands and knees, while Pierre screamed at me. 'Show me the tongue. Naturally, I didn't want to, I was afraid, but he forced me. He said if I didn't do what he wanted, he'd go to my father and say I'd been feeling up Janine, the school whore. Well you can imagine, that would have been the most dreadful thing. You see, I was the son of the local priest and it would have brought such shame on my family. Well, Pierre, really was a dirty pig. He stood in a corner and he unzipped his pants and taking out his dick he masturbated himself into a fever as he watched me execute all sorts of antics. He made me lap at a plate of milk, saying the tongue reminded him of a cat. I had to lap away at the plate and lick it entirely clean before he was happy, then he made me manipulate my tongue in all sorts of crude poses. Pierre was cruel and more than a little twisted. Last of all, he caught my tongue in his fingers and, although I was gagging, he stretched it out and looked at it closely, and I have to say, that really hurt. 'My God!' he said. 'Can you be real? You must have fallen from space and be an alien to have such a weird tool.' Well, my eyes were watering and I thought I was going to choke. That's when Janine leapt on him. She must have been watching us, because I heard this screech like a wild cat and the next thing I knew, Pierre had let me go and he was dancing around and around with Janine clinging to his back like a monkey, slapping his head and biting at his ears. My God, she was quite a wild woman, and the first love of my life.'

'That's terrible.' I said, hardly able to believe it. An episode that horrible could mark you for life.'

'Oh that's so true.' Marius continued. 'The tongue has been a curse, it has also been a blessing. In this instance, I caught your attention, didn't I?' Leaning forward he rubbed at my mouth with his thumb. 'Well, that horrible experience was my grand – coming out – so to speak. Janine had a queer look in her luminous, tear-filled eyes; it was like a madness, mingled with desire. I found her compassion so arousing as she untied me. 'Poor thing,' she said, stroking my hair like she might her pet cat. 'He's a perverted animal, that Pierre. You know, I saw it, I saw your tongue, Marius. But will you show it to me now, all of it. In private. It's not that I want to make fun of it. I just love the sight of your tool. I find your tongue so hot and erotic and it does crazy and wonderful things to me inside here.' She stroked her mound through her skirt.

Well, I didn't know what to do. Janine was a gorgeous girl, all curves and oozing ripe sex. I didn't believe a word of those rumours about her; she was simply blessed like me with a physiological peculiarity, in her case incredibly huge tits. Since she didn't drop her knickers for just anyone, the boys ribbed her like crazy, I guess they were jealous because they wanted to get their hands on her and Janine wouldn't accommodate them. As I stared at her, I could see her tight little nipples straining away, as her blouse could hardly contain those huge appendages. Janine's buttons were always ready to pop. I shot out my tongue and leaning forward Janine stared at it. 'Oh, I love your tongue, it's so pink and it looks just like the tongue of my kitten. Yes that's what I shall call you from now on, Langue de chat. At first I wondered if she was making a joke about it but when she moved forward and began unbuttoning her blouse I could tell that she was deadly serious. 'Wouldn't you like to lick on these, my delicious Langue de chat.'

You can guess what happened, it turned out that on this occasion I was the cat that got the cream. I lapped and sucked away at the huge round globes and as I fondled and titillated her shell pink nipples, Janine orgasmed time and time again and that was even before I set to work on her cunt. One thing you'll discover – I'm blessed with great patience. I worked away tirelessly on Janine until I'd licked away every last drop of her pussy cream and made her come so many times I lost count. On that day, I was reborn as I realised my tongue had some fabulously dirty uses. Uses that made women scream and faint with lust.'

Marius poked out the tip of his pink tongue, licked his lips and then pushed it out to its furthest extremity. It was smooth, pink and extremely plump. 'I have a piercing what do you think?' He wriggled the appendage and I saw the glisten of a silver tongue stud. 'Why don't you come a little bit closer and taste me.'

I couldn't stop thinking of the tongue licking my breast as it had Janine's and I shivered as I imagined its slow progression down my body and between my legs. Now as I stared at it, the tongue wriggled like a particularly appetising worm on the end of a hook and I don't know what came over me because lunging forward I fastened my lips to Marius's. Laughing, he pulled me to my feet. 'Come along, I have a little place not far from here.'

I was too excited to resist as Marius and I tumbled through his apartment door. He pushed me against the wall while his hand slipped under my skirt, and the tip of his lingual acrobat began exploring my face. I opened my mouth in invitation and it came rushing in like an express train, my own tongue darting forward to intercept it, jousting and dancing.

I was trembling so much with excitement Marius had to undress me himself. He did this with great skill, loosening my buttons, tweaking and pinching my nipples as my garments fell to the floor in a tangled heap. Naked, we then tumbled onto his futon and he lay pressed against me for a moment, showing me his tongue, dancing it about and thrusting it out to its full length, while his cock – which was almost as meaty as his other tool – nuzzled my thigh. Angelina was right, amazingly, Langue de chat's tongue was much longer than a dick. In fact, it was simply incredible.

I was behaving like a whore but I couldn't control myself. The oral muscle was driving me wild. Gripping my breasts in my hands, I offered them up, like a sacrifice to the stiff, pink tongue. 'Lick me, Langue de chat.' I commanded.

'It's very strong, feel how strong it is.' Taking my finger Marius made me hold the fleshy appendage. 'Did you ever feel a muscle like that? You know, I train it and this tongue is now so strong it can go for ever. I bet you can't wait to have it, giving you satisfaction up your cunt.'

I was writhing with desire as the tongue began to dance over my feverish body. Marius used it with sexual finesse, rotating it over my breasts, flicking it against my nipples, then treating me to a delicious tongue bath, as he worked his way further and further down towards my hot sex and bucking hips. I cried and moaned and crumpled the bed sheets in my fists as I begged him for satisfaction but, pinning my arms to the bed, he laughed. 'You mustn't rush; you must allow the tongue to pleasure you.'

'I can't wait, I want it now. Push it inside me. I want to experience it licking and sucking every inch of me.'

'You are far too excitable. I intend this to be a multi-orgasmic event, my darling,' he whispered in my ear. Now just do as I say.'

'Anything,' I whispered, gritting my teeth. 'Just stick it in.'

'I can tell you, babe, after this you'll never want cock again.' Marius grinned and holding open my plump, peachy sex lips, he snuggled down between my legs and, with the balls of his thumbs, began pressing on each side of my oozing mound, darting the tip of the monster tongue into my cunt and jabbing at the sensitive flesh with sharp arrow like movements of the oral gymnast. Just when I thought it couldn't get any better, he forced apart my lubricious sex slick thighs and commenced sucking with great intensity on my now throbbing clit, his saucy pink impostor penis, dancing up and down my slit, insistently circling my swollen cherry, as I shuddered and moaned and raised my hips.

Langue de chat was a lingual magician and he delivered satisfaction with tantalising precision to the point of sensory overload. Tongue is so much better than cock; after all a tongue can change shape and texture from excitably smooth and flexible, to devilishly rough and muscular and what is more, it can creep into every forbidden little crack and crevice, finding those tricky erogenous zones most men can never locate. The cunnilingual seducer soon found my G spot, the elusive trigger to my sexual satisfaction, and it bore down with such a mad fluttering I was instantly catapulted into a thrashing crescendo of orgasmic release.

And I can tell you, the cunnilingual pleasure did not stop there, but kept on coming as the incredible elastic tool crept further up inside my velvet pussy until Marius was so deeply pressed in my moist cunt, his lips were nibbling my sex. Opening his mouth, he began to devour my juicy mound with purrs of pleasure as his hands energetically squeezed my flesh. He was now treating both my tingling G spot and my grasping cunt to a thoroughly salacious massage, his energetic elastic performer undertaking a skilful gymnastic routine, lunging and rotating like an acrobat on a trapeze, as it worked away with machine like efficiency on my sex.

By this time, I was practically insensate with lust and I had experienced such orgasmic satisfaction, I felt as if the tongue had turned me inside out and examined every centimetre of my intimate sexual places with the thoroughness of a surgeon. Playfully, I tried pushing Langue de chat away with my foot and he bobbed up smiling at me. 'Oh are you tired already, my darling?' He flicked the tongue back and forwards over his sex-wet mouth. 'Well, what a shame, because I've only just started. You know I love the taste of pussy, there's nothing quite like it and I intend to taste each bit of you.' Slithering up my body, he squeezed my breast and I felt his penis slide greedily into my grasping hole. Then he began to investigate my mouth with the same thoroughness he had ravaged my cunt.

Langue de chat has taken the phrase – tongue action – and elevated it to a whole new level. Now, cock will never be enough for me and I doubt any other man will ever be able to live up to my impossibly exacting oral standards.

Langue de chat has fallen in love with me and he tells me he wants to keep feeding on my cunt in order to exercise and give the muscular invader enough of a workout to maintain its acrobatic flexibility. Well, I'm certainly game for that and, what is more, I can let you into a secret, as I am now taking lessons in tongue craft, from Langue de chat so I can repay the favour on his equally naughty dick. My motto now is. 'Who needs penis when tongue is best', especially if the tongue craft is performed by Langue de chat.

Molly's New Mistress
by Lilli Lace

Molly was freshly shaved for this occasion. Mr Chester, who had acquired her services from Madam Almeda's House, called her into the gigantic master bedroom of his summer lake house. Before the balcony window overlooking his private estate, before the eyes of the world, he told her to strip completely naked and lie on the edge of the canopied bed with her knees bent and her legs apart. She obeyed, and as she removed her short summer dress and cotton bra and panties, she felt Mr Chester's eyes running up and down her body. They took in the smooth curve of her full buttocks and travelled up to her swelling breasts which were partially obscured by her mousy brown curls. Never in her life had she felt more desirable. When she laid back on the silk sheets and lifted her legs to the desired position, Mr Chester took a good long look at his new purchase and Molly saw the bulge in his trousers.

He was in his business suit, the suit in which she had first seen him at Madam Almeda's house when he had come to look around. On her first day there, the other more experienced girls had forewarned her that not all the gentlemen that came to Madam Almeda's House were just as gentlemanly in bed, and Molly had secretly been thrilled to learn this. This was, after all, the reason she had left her stuffy college comforts and boring studies. She had hoped that, by working at Madam Almeda's House, lounging around the scarlet sitting room and talking with the other much more self-assured, seductive creatures who surrounded her, that she might be provided with the opportunities to fulfil her secret sexual night-time fantasies. She looked up to these women, the attention that they commanded, the spellbinding way in which they walked and held themselves, as though they couldn't care less if a man was interested in them or not. What mattered was whether or not *she* was interested in *him* and, if she was, then she would let him know it and he would be a lucky man indeed!

Molly had become bored with the inexperienced young men who, in her previous life, had come calling at the dorm for her. They were eager to please but not where it mattered. She felt that they simply wanted to take from her, never stopping to find out what she might want. Her fantasies were probably their ultimate fantasies but not ones they would be willing to act out. They would probably only discuss them with their friends and pretend to one another with lewd laughter and jokes, a lot of shoving and pushing and leg-pulling, that they would be up for a perverse thrill if ever the opportunity arose. Molly knew they probably wouldn't know what to do if it ever did, so she turned her back on those sexually inadequate boys and, after months of deliberation, she finally plucked up the courage to shun her studies and seek employment with Madam Almeda's House. However, it took a week of waiting and posing in the skimpy outfits she had been provided with, before she found her man. It was Mr Chester. His brooding eyes and stately air, not to mention his beautifully tailored suit, slicked back hair and shiny leather shoes suggested that maybe, *just maybe* he could provide the kind of sexual excitement she had been searching for. When he walked into the room with the short, round, Madam Almeda, he projected authority and Molly was dying to know if this authoritarian attitude might be transferred to the bedroom, so she draped herself on the red velvet sofa in the elegant lounge in her shortest negligee and stared at him intently until his eyes met hers. Molly felt herself radiating with an untapped sensuality. Whether he thought this was intentional or not did not matter to her. It worked. He pointed her out to Madam Almeda and offered to take her to his lake house there and then.

The whole journey home he did not touch her. In the back of the chauffeur-driven Jaguar, she gazed at him intently, but he did not say a word to her, he only stared ahead, lost in his own thoughts. She was only slightly perplexed but she supposed this was the way the game was supposed to be played until they got behind closed doors. Once they reached his beautiful lake house, Molly did not even have time to look around. Mr Chester simply ushered her upstairs into the master bedroom and Molly thought he must be rushing so that he could have his way with her before his wife found out. That's if he was even married. Molly hadn't even thought of this but she assumed it would be breaking some unspoken rule if she asked him if he was married or not so she decided not to say anything at all. His rushing her made her doubt her earlier assumption of him. Maybe he wasn't the kind of man she was hoping he would be. Perhaps he was simply going to use her and have done with her in the space of half an hour or so. She felt her fantasies slipping away …

Everything was all quickly thrust to the back of Molly's mind however, when they entered the luxurious bedroom. Mr Chester removed his suit jacket and produced some shaving cream. Once undressed and in the indicated position, on her back, legs up, knees bent, Molly felt herself brimming with the kind of carnal excitement which she had previously been forced to lock tight away back at home. She gasped as the cold lather was applied between her parted legs and she had to stop herself from laughing and pushing him away when he used a soft shaving brush to spread the foam all over her exposed area. Then, very carefully, he began to shave her, his fingers moving around her and, much to Molly's pleasure, inside her, gently pulling the young skin taut so that the razor could glide over and around her delicate pussy. When he was finished, he washed her using the water from the basin on the bedside table and then dried her, removing the remaining foam slowly with a soft, fluffy towel to reveal her soft, pink bud.

He could have had her there and then, God knows she was wet enough, but instead he had grabbed her ankles and in one swift motion pulled her around so that her head was resting on the pillows and her feet faced the foot of the bed. He then produced some restraints from under the bed and proceeded to cuff her wrists and ankles to the bedposts. Molly was enjoying this too much to object; it was more than what she had expected from her first encounter with a patron of Almeda's House but then, to her astonishment, instead of taking off his own clothes and mounting her as she had expected, he simply walked over and opened the bedroom door and called in his wife.

She entered in her thin robe and Molly could see her forty-something body long and lean beneath. When she disrobed she was clad only in a tiny black lace thong. Her breasts were firm, her olive skim gleamed and her eyes and hair were dark and tumultuous. She eyed the pale young girl on the bed hungrily and then began to crawl on top of her while Mr Chester sat himself in a chair by the wall and watched. The other woman's body felt strange straddling her own. Mrs Chester bent her head and her full lips began to suck on Molly's left nipple. Molly moaned. She couldn't help it. After seconds, her right nipple started to *ache* for some attention and Molly gently thrust her right breast towards those full lips, but she was firmly pushed back onto the bed. Mrs Chester's hand which had pushed her back hovered over her right breast for a moment and then cheekily tweaked her nipple, causing Molly to gasp, before it slid down to feel the wetness between her legs as Mrs Chester continued to suck on her left nipple. Her fingers played between Molly's legs, stroking her up and down. The bare patch between Molly's legs was smooth and more sensitive to Mrs Chester's insistent touch. Her silky tongue which was quickly circulating the hard rosy tip of Molly's nipple really was getting to be too much. How the right nipple *ached* for that same attention.

Quite suddenly, Mrs Chester left Molly's nipple and gently kissed her way down her young, lithe body, down over her swelled breasts, over her navel, her tongue circulating round Molly's belly button, licking the salty perspiration which had gathered on her smooth tummy and then further down between her legs. Here she paused, and then began sucking sensuously on Molly's creamy inner thighs, slowly alternating between the naked quivering flesh of one thigh and then moving on to the trembling flesh of the other. Then, Molly watched with inexperienced eyes as two slender fingers slowly parted her pussy lips and the older woman's tongue gently prodded her exposed clit and then started to lap away at her naked pussy with long languorous strokes, like a cat with its cream. At first Molly had been too surprised at Mrs Chester's sudden appearance to think, but she had quickly realised that Mr Chester had brought her here for his wife's pleasure and instead of being angry at the deception, instead she found that she was actually excited by this experience which previously she could only have dreamed about. Molly tore her gaze away from the woman kneeling between her legs and glanced at Mr Chester. He was sitting with his legs crossed and the tips of his fingers steeped together before him. He was concentrating on his wife, her thong-clad rump thrust into the air, her long dark hair brushing Molly's plump thighs and her tongue licking languorously away between Molly's parted lips. How Molly wished he would get up and smack his wife's round firm arse, forcing her to pleasure Molly faster, maybe even join them himself, taking his wife from behind with his long, firm shaft. Molly was so turned on by this thought that she was willing Mr Chester to look at her, to read her mind. Suddenly, Mrs Chester sat up and grasping one of her own breasts she brought it down to Molly's pussy and tickled the moist insides of Molly's parted lips with her hardened nipple. Molly groaned and, turning back to the older woman, she tried to rub herself against Mrs Chester's plump breast but Mrs Chester was having none of it. Again she pushed Molly's naked body down onto the sheets. She lowered her head and carefully found the little groove of her clit with her tongue and started to work on it like a woman possessed. Molly could feel her own wetness running down the inside of her thighs to the groove between her buttocks as with successive little, lizard-like vibrations of her tongue Mrs Chester concentrated wholly on this one little spot. Molly felt helpless. She wanted to push the older woman from her as the tip of her tongue was overpowering her bare little clit, but she couldn't. Instead, she pulled at her restraints, bucking her hips to and from those parted lips. She did not cry out for her to stop either – the power of authority that Molly had been raised to respect and never disobey was too deeply ingrained within her – but it also added to the excitement. Even if Molly cried out, she knew that Mrs Chester was not a woman to take orders, she was a woman in a position of power, backed by an equally powerful husband, who had to be obeyed and this turned Molly on more than anything as she watched her new mistress pleasuring her body. Mrs Chester grabbed her buttocks, each peach in each of her hands, and forced Molly to her mouth so that she could no longer wriggle around, but had to stay as she was, at the mercy of that demon tongue. The pleasure was excruciating and Molly came hard and fast, her body shuddering and seizing, half raised from the bed. Mrs Chester raised her head and looked at her husband lustfully while Molly started to subside before her. He made a signal with his hand which Molly barely registered as she was too busy feeling the residual pleasure wash over her body. Mrs Chester turned back to Molly who was breathing heavily, trying to lower her exhausted body to the bed thinking she was done for now, but instead Mrs Chester kept Molly's arse firmly raised in a vice-like grip and, like a lioness, she lowered her head and began to devour Molly all over again.

The Ex Factor
by Sophia Valenti

I'll admit it; I did miss my ex, but she and I weren't right for each other and we both knew it. Our breakup didn't result in overwhelming heartache, but to have it happen the night before Valentine's Day was rough. So the next day, on an evening when everyone I knew was coupled up and out on the town, I was watching television and feeling a little lonely. I knew I had to try to make the best of it and swore to enjoy myself as best I could – but then I received a phone call that wound up making my resolution a whole lot easier to keep.

The call was from Kevin, an old flame of mine. Back in the day, we'd had a kinky affair that began as a red-hot free-for-all but had gradually fizzled out, however, we were still close – and I did occasionally fantasize about him. I'm only human, after all, and the sex had been pretty spectacular. These days, Kevin and I talk regularly and see each other whenever our busy schedules allow. We like to say that we have the best once-every-five-weeks friendship there is, each of us intuitively knowing exactly what the other needs. That certainly wound up being the case that night, though it wasn't how I'd originally thought the evening would unfold.

Kevin surprised me with his call, announcing that he was in the neighbourhood with his new girlfriend, Mia, and wanted to introduce me to her. Given my situation, I welcomed the distraction of company. I was also eager to meet Mia, since Kevin had previously spoken so highly of her. The fact that he wanted to introduce her to me – and on Valentine's Day, no less – meant that he must really like her and that she'd be sticking around for a while.

And when I answered my door a short time later, I knew exactly why. Mia was gorgeous! With jet-black hair that hung past her shoulders, emerald-green eyes and a bright smile, she was absolutely captivating, and her shapely figure didn't hurt her cause either. Her red slip dress was so thin and delicate it enhanced rather than hid her body. Mia was runway-model tall, but unlike those scarecrow-like waifs, Mia had miles of curves that had me transfixed. She was beautifully proportioned with pillowy breasts, a tapered waist and sensuously full hips. I tried to behave, but I couldn't stop myself; before Kevin had a chance to make our introductions, my eyes were roaming up and down her body like those of a predatory animal. However, what was even more surprising was the way she seemed to return my interest with a lustful look of her own. The flash in her eyes was brief, but it was enough to make me ponder what sort of thoughts were racing through her head; I hoped they were as naughty as mine. But a second later that sensuous spark had vanished and was replaced by a sweet, playful look which led me to wonder if I'd imagined the whole exchange.

I'd just met Mia, and I didn't want her thinking I was some sort of sex-crazed maniac, so I tried to push the episode – and my sinfully delicious thoughts – out of my mind as pleasantries were exchanged. Kevin mentioned that they'd seen a movie at the nearby theatre, and he'd wanted to stop in and see how I was doing. His words were laced with a tenderness that I found touching. He knew all about the breakup, of course, and he was doing his friendly duty by checking in on me. I appreciated his concern, but I assured them both that while I had no regrets, I was also ready to move on.

"Well, then," he said, "that's a reason to celebrate!" Celebrate was Kevin's code word for liquor. The look on his face – the broad smile, raised eyebrows and wide-open eyes – made me laugh out loud.

"Don't worry, hot shot," I told him. "I was about to offer you guys some wine, but I was going to let you take a seat first!" I shook my head in mock dismay at Kevin and then turned to Mia, gesturing toward the couch in my effort to be a proper hostess. "Please, make yourself comfortable."

"Thanks," she said as she settled into the velvet-covered sofa, crossing one long, tanned leg over the other. As she and I appraised each other once again, I sensed a hint of appreciation – laced with just the right amount of wickedness – and that realization made my heart beat faster. I didn't think I was imagining things this time. I nervously rubbed my hands against my jeans; my palms were sweaty and my fingers were itching to roam her curves. In my mind, I was already peeling off her skimpy dress, cupping her breasts in my hands and lavishing those luscious mounds with kisses. Ah, well, so much for controlling my dirty mind.

"All I've got is a nice cheap red – that okay with you guys?" I asked as I headed into the kitchen, hoping to diffuse the sensual tension that seemed to be developing between me and Kevin's girl.

"Mmm, cheap wine, my favourite," Kevin said, his words followed by the sound of Mia's musical laughter. He still seemed unaware of connection that she and I had made, but if things continued on the path that I was imagining, he wouldn't be in the dark for long. But from what I remembered about Kevin, I doubted that he would find it a problem.

In the kitchen, I took a deep breath and gathered my bearings, then hunted down a corkscrew. Normally, I'm a very cool and collected person, but there was something about Mia that lit a fire in me. I wasn't used to feeling that way so soon after meeting someone, and the fact that I did made me apprehensive and turned me on all at the same time. I managed to work out some of my nervous energy as I wrestled with the corkscrew and bottle, feeling satisfied when I heard the telltale pop of the cork pulling free. I was filling the third glass when Kevin snuck into the kitchen and sidled up to me.

"So, whaddya thing of Mia?" he asked in a not-so-hushed whisper, picking up one of the glasses and taking a sip of wine – well, more of a gulp, really.

"You'd better watch it, Kevin," I teased, looked at him from under half-lidded eyes. "You bring such a sweet piece into my place and expect me to keep my hands to myself?"

"Who said you had to keep you hands to yourself?" Mia said slyly. Kevin and I both jumped with surprise. We'd had no idea she'd followed him, but there she was standing in the doorway, looking even more delicious and tempting than she had appeared when I'd first laid eyes on her.

Mia's body was illuminated from behind by the bright lamplight coming from the living room. Through the thin fabric of her dress, I could see the outline of her plush body and my mouth watered. I found myself transfixed by the glowing light that emanated from between her parted thighs. Mia rested one hand on her cocked hip, while the other dangled at her side. Her head was tilted inquisitively as she awaited a response from either of us, but none

175

came.

Kevin and I were still too startled to speak, so Mia took control of the situation. She sashayed into the kitchen with a feline-like stroll, her hips swaying enticingly and the click-clack of her stilettos on the tile floor mesmerizing me with their sexy Morse code. She looked me up and down in a way that – this time – gave no doubt as to what sort of thoughts she was thinking: They were definitely dirty.

Kevin's mouth quirked into a bemused smile that I had a feeling I was mirroring. Mia reached out her hand and took the wineglass from her boyfriend. Her delicate fingers wrapped around the stem, and she brought the glass to her lips, looking at me above its rim as she slowly sipped the ruby liquid.

I licked my lips nervously, and as I admired her luscious figure, my excitement ratcheted up exponentially with each passing second. Mia handed the glass back to Kevin and moved closer to me. I was breathing through slightly parted lips as she reached up and brushed my hair back, pushing my auburn curls away from my face and over my shoulders. She was standing so close to that I could smell the wine on her breath.

"Kevin," she said softly but with a playfully chastising tone, "you didn't tell me your friend was so pretty." Mia was speaking to him, but she was looking directly at me. She was considering me so carefully, studying me so intensely, that every nerve ending in my body seemed to tingle. She'd barely touched me, and I was already feeling faint with desire. My breasts were rising and falling erratically with each panting breath, and the cool breeze drifting in through the window did nothing to cool my ardour. I couldn't hold back any longer and reached out, my fingers grazing her bare shoulder and briefly trailing down her arm. Her skin was so soft and warm that I let out a little sigh of contentment when I made contact with her. Upon hearing the sound, Mia's glossy pink lips curled upward. It would have been too easy to sweep her up in my arms for a passionate kiss, but since we were most certainly not alone, I had to address my friend. After all, as tempting as Mia was, I had no intention of leaving him out of the fun.

"So, Kevin," I said, momentarily tearing my eyes away from Mia's. "I hope the two of you don't have other plans for tonight. I'd love it if you could stay awhile."

"N-no, no plans," Kevin stammered.

"Well, *I* have plans," Mia added, wandering over to stroke Kevin's face, teasing his cheek with her red-lacquered nails. He seemed to melt instantly, looking every bit the submissive that I recalled him being. Mia, on the other hand, seemed to grow even bolder, turning toward me and saying, "And I hope you can help me with them, Belinda."

"I think I can I do that," I answered in a hushed whisper.

"Good," Mia answered, her voice still strong. "Let's head someplace a little more comfortable, shall we?"

There was no reason to delay any longer; all pretence was gone. I took Mia's hand and led her to my bedroom, with Kevin following behind us at a polite distance. I flicked on a lamp in the corner of the room, the ambient lighting casting us in a soft, sexy glow. Mia ordered Kevin to get naked. He immediately obeyed, neatly folding each item of clothing and placing it on a nearby chair. As he stripped, Mia gave me her undivided attention. She leaned toward me and our mouths met in a slow, sensuous kiss. Our gloss-slick lips slid against each other as we embraced. Her body was deliciously soft, and

I savoured the feeling of her plush breasts pressing against my own. All of that perfumed female flesh grinding against me made my pussy ache with longing.

All of my earlier fantasies came to life as I slid my hands down her sides, enjoying the feel of her rounded breasts, nipped waist and flared hips. My hands stopped at her thighs while our kisses grew more frenzied. Our tongues tangled wildly as my fingers gathered up her silky dress, balling up the fabric in my fists and causing her hem to rise higher and higher on her thighs. We reluctantly broke apart so I could lift her delicate shift off her body, but before I tasted those delicious lips again I had to admire her naked form. Mia wore no underwear, and she looked even more beautiful standing there in only her high-heeled shoes with all of her charms on display. Her heavy breasts were topped with thick brown nipples that were already erect and beckoning me to lick them. Her legs were long and toned, and her mound was covered with a light dusting of dark hair. I kissed her one more time on the mouth before I lavished her sumptuous tits with wet kisses. After nuzzling her sweet cleavage, I circled one rubbery nipple with my tongue and then took it between my lips and flicked it with my tongue tip. Mia brought her hands to my hair, tangling her fingers in my tresses and pulling me tighter to her body, forcing more of her fulsome flesh between my lips. She uttered wordless moans of pleasure as I then teased the other nub in a similar way. As I enjoyed the feel of her nipple under my tongue, I peeked at Kevin out of the corner of my eye. He was standing a few feet away, with his hands dutifully behind his back and his semi-hard cock bobbing in front of him. His brown eyes were wide with admiration. I knew we would have even more fun once we allowed him to join us.

I pulled back from Mia, leaving both of her nipples glistening and swollen. By this point, her chest and face were flushed, and she was breathing heavily. She glanced at her boyfriend, and she seemed pleased by his continued obedience. Then she set herself to the task of stripping me. Although she seemed wildly turned on, she took her time revealing my body. As she slipped off my T-shirt, unhooked my lacy bra and slid down my jeans, she made sure to drag her fingers against my tingling flesh. She wasn't merely undressing me; she was caressing me and stripping me with a sensual intent, her eyes alight with lust as each inch of my body was revealed to her – and Kevin. I gathered from the increasingly erect state of his dick that he was enjoying the show. He was a good boy, though, and wouldn't move from his spot until he was summoned. I wasn't entirely sure what Mia had planned for us, but I was willing to let her be our kinky ringmaster for the evening.

By the time I was down to my panties, the ache in my sex had transformed into a pulsing, insistent beat. Mia urged me backward until I hit the bed, and I laughed as I tumbled onto the mattress, my legs splaying open. My laughter was cut short, however, when Mia gripped the sides of my undies and yanked them down my thighs. The tiny garment was soaked with the evidence of my arousal, and I blushed as my wet sex was suddenly exposed to my new lover. Mia couldn't take her eyes off my glistening cunt.

"Perfect," she muttered in a barely audible whisper. She seemed to be talking to herself more than anyone else. "Kevin, come here. Belinda would like something to suck on while I tease this little pussy of hers."

Kevin scurried over to the bed, positioning himself so I could reach his cock with little effort. I parted my lips and welcomed him inside my mouth. I placed a hand on his thigh to steady myself and slid my lips down his length at the same time that Mia's tongue skidded along my slit. She rummaged in my slippery folds, causing me to buck my hips toward her face. When she flicked my clit, I moaned around Kevin's stiff rod, the vibrations of my utterances giving him unspeakable pleasure. His body quivered as he struggled to remain still and let me work him at my own pace. As Mia whipped me into a frenzy, I took him down deep, swallowing until I felt his shaft pulsing in my throat and my nose was buried in his dark pubic hair. He stroked my face gently as I bobbed my mouth along the length of his dick at a more rapid pace. It was such a heady moment, to be sucking my ex's cock while his pretty new girlfriend was tonguing me nearly to the point of orgasm.

I was on the verge of tumbling over the edge and moaning wildly around Kevin's prick when Mia suddenly pulled back from my pussy. My groan of disappointment was muffled by the cock in my mouth, but I knew that Mia wouldn't leave me hanging. I momentarily stopped sucking on Kevin, but I continued to stroke his slick erection as Mia, her lips shiny with my juices, uttered her next breathy statement.

"Belinda, please tell me you have some naughty toys."

Wordlessly, I pointed to the nightstand, and Mia crawled across the bed and yanked open the drawer. With a gleeful look on her face, she reached inside and pulled out a strap-on dildo. She quickly affixed the harness around her hips and positioned herself once again between my spread thighs. The bright pink cock bobbing from her pelvis looked deliciously obscene, and as she held the toy steady so she could run its head up and down my slit, I closed my eyes to savour the sensation and resumed my efforts on Kevin's unflagging dick.

Mia shoved the faux cock into my dripping cunt with one hard thrust. As she pounded into me, I rocked my hips upward to meet her, wanting even more. My ass beat a steady tattoo against the mattress with the rhythm of our fucking. I don't know how I managed to keep Kevin's dick in my mouth; it was as if I was on cock-sucking autopilot. Over the noise of Mia's hips slapping against mine and the squishy sounds of her cock plunging in and out of my wet sex, I could hear Kevin's whimpers and moans of pleasure. I reached up and stroked his balls, tickling them with my fingernails and making him jerk wildly. At the same time, Mia shoved the toy into me as far as it would go and began to grind her hips against mine, no doubt enjoying the friction of the toy against her own clit as much as I enjoyed being filled by it.

Mia had been fucking me so energetically that her face and body were glistening with perspiration and strands of her long hair were stuck to her face. I couldn't get enough; I was being stuffed at both ends, and I loved it. All too soon, though, she yanked her dick out of my hole. I was so wet that I felt like I'd left a puddle on the mattress underneath my ass. Mia moved from between my legs and motioned to Kevin, breathlessly ordering him to take her place and pleasure me.

I gasped in ecstasy when I felt his familiar cock plunge inside me. The toy had been nice, but there's nothing like a hot, hard dick. I bent my legs and hugged him with my thighs, meeting him thrust for thrust. At that point, I felt the mattress shift. That's when I realized Mia was positioning herself behind Kevin. Still pumping his dick into me, he glanced over his shoulder.

"You keep doing what you were told," Mia said

sharply. "You take care of Belinda – and I'll take care of your ass," she added, punctuating her words with a sharp slap to his butt that drove his cock into me to the root. Kevin groaned at her announcement, but he didn't protest. In fact, he seemed to work himself into me faster and harder.

Mia peppered his back with kisses, travelling down his spine. At one point she completely disappeared from my view. I couldn't tell what she was doing, but I felt her hands on my thighs as she continued her journey. Kevin gasped, and I had a feeling Mia was teasing his asshole – whether with her fingers or her tongue, I didn't know – getting him ready to accept her cock. It was such a dirty idea, to have her fuck his ass while he was plunging his dick in and out of me. The thought made me shiver with indecent pleasure.

I knew the exact moment she worked the head of her toy into his back hole. Kevin groaned and shivered, dropping his weight onto my body and plunging his dick into me. His groan turned into one long moan as Mia slid her body up against his and her face appeared over his shoulder. She winked and me as she wriggled behind Kevin. When she finally worked the length of the toy completely into him, she stroked his side and whispered endearments as he shivered between our bodies.

Mia gave Kevin a chance to get used to being so thoroughly invaded, holding herself still so he could get acclimated to the sensation. As he took long, deep breaths, I squeezed his dick with my pussy, feeling him pulse in response to my intimate massage.

"You're doing so good, my pet. Are you ready for more?" Mia asked gently.

Kevin, unable to speak, simply nodded. Mia pulled back slowly, and he exited my cunt at the same time. And when Mia thrust her dick back into his ass, he mimicked her motion, sending his dick deep into my tingling sex. After a few clumsy motions, the two of them developed a nice steady rhythm, to the point where it nearly seemed that Mia was fucking me herself with each fluid motion of her hips. I was so deliciously pinned against the mattress that I could barely move, but that was fine with me. I was the happy recipient of Kevin's hard cock, having missed the sensation of being fucked by a guy. The three of us were bucking and moaning and writhing in a lusty tangle of limbs, furiously working our way to climax.

Although I couldn't see their point of connection, the knowledge that Mia was pounding Kevin's ass was quickly bringing me to the edge. That combined with the sensation of his thrusting dick and the friction of his pelvis against my clit sparked my release, and as the pleasure washed over me, my cunt spasmed around Kevin's cock. He followed me shortly afterward, burying his face in my shoulder as he released a series of wordless moans and shot his load. He collapsed most of his weight on top of me, with his dick still nestled in my pussy, as Mia took her pleasure by reaming his back hole. I concentrated on her face, which wore a mask of absolute ecstasy as she bucked into him one last time and came with a triumphant shout.

Afterward, as we lay together in a breathless heap, Kevin spoke up. "So, Belinda, you never answered my question. What do you think of Mia?"

I looked from her smiling face to his and said, "I think she's a keeper."

That Kevin, he always knows exactly what I need.

Katy Keene, Teen Detective
by Lynn Lake

It was a high-pitched scream that awoke Katy Keene that fateful Saturday morning – her dad discovering that his beloved, brand-new, riding mower had gone missing from their garage.

The red-headed tomboy turned heartthrob was on the case in an instant. Three bookcases full of Nancy Drew mystery novels, a shelf full of Zodiac P.I. mangas, a spinning rack of *CSI* DVDs, and a laptop loaded with detecting games, attested to the eighteen year-old's avid interest and informal training in the art and science of sleuthing.

But that was all on paper and pixel. Now, at last, she could actually put theory into practice.

Katy jumped in and out of the shower. Then wriggled into a pair of pink shorty-shorts and a 'Clue You!' T-shirt, dipping her sparkly-tipped toes into a pair of white sneakers and staring determinedly at her pretty, freckled face in the mirror. As she braided her copper-coloured hair into twin pigtails,

she took a deep breath, so excited her nipples poked out of her tee and her pussy stayed moist in her shorts. And, then, she sprang into action: Katy Keene, Teen Detective.

First, she intently listened to her father blubber out his discovery of the mower theft – and a detailed description of the missing Toro Classic GT/315-8 – to the overworked local Sheriff's Department on the telephone. Taking notes, and taking names. Because all the police could promise was: 'to look into the matter'.

Next, Katy polished off a bowl of Fruit Loops and stuffed her 'FBI' backpack full of forensic tools (her Nancy Drew detective kit). Then left the house to get her bike out of the garage. Her father was standing looking at the empty spot where his riding mower had been parked. He'd forgotten to lock the garage door the previous night, again.

Katy gave the distraught man a consoling hug and then walked her bike out on to the long driveway that led to the rural road out front. The hot summer sun blazed down on her smooth, slender arms and legs, adding a new layer of tan and dew to the dusting of hair on her youthful limbs.

She was ten feet down the driveway, scouring the asphalt with her big blue eyes, when she noticed a small clump of dried dirt that had once been mud. Like the mud on the tyres of Dad's riding mower, after he'd been cutting down by the pond yesterday evening.

She examined the lump of dirt with her magnifying glass and pair of tweezers, then dropped it into a baggy – to be definitely matched up with the pond edge earth later on. Then she smiled and nodded, eyes and hair glinting under the sun, squinting at the vague trail of flung-off mud that led down the driveway and out onto the road.

She hopped on her bike and peddled slowly away, following the dried mud clues. Concluding that the perp hadn't pushed the mower out of the garage and loaded it onto a waiting getaway pick-up or van, but rather had pushed it out to the road and then ridden it away.

The dirty trail ended at Timothy X Gruder's front

lawn, a half-mile down the road.

A lawn that was normally wildly overgrown with grass and weeds, testament to the eccentric man's commitment to all things organic; but which was now neatly cut!

Katy was busily taking grass blade samples, measuring cut depth and blade angles, when Timothy found her crouched down on his front lawn. "Hey, little lady, whatcha up to?" the environmental beanpole with the hippy complex asked, looking down at the teenager's delicately curved back – where her shorts rode low and tee high, and her brown skin was exposed.

Katy jumped to her feet, sealing the baggy of grass blades. "Your lawn seems in unusually good order all of a sudden, Mr Gruder," she commented dryly.

Timothy rubbed his large, bony hands on his patched-up bell-bottoms. "Right on. I got an order from the county to clean it up – or get fined." He shoved his granny glasses back up his long nose. "Hey, man, you don't think I lifted your dad's riding mower, do you?"

Katy tightly gripped the straps of her backpack, making her cupcake boobs stick out even more, nipples pointing hard and accusing at her neighbour. "You've complained about the noise and gasoline consumption of such lawn-care devices before, I believe. Perhaps, as an act of–"

"Hey, that's heavy, sweet mama," Timothy protested, his eyes losing their natural glaze as he fully appraised the teen hottie. "Here, come with me – I'll show you I'm clean."

Katy shadowed the man back to the tool-shed in behind his chartreuse-painted house. The small wood and hemp structure was crammed full of everything from scythes to sledgehammers, but no riding mower. Katy cleared a spot on the workbench that ran along one wall and hopped aboard, balancing her 'Police' writing pad on a bare leg and making notes. Knowing that any fibres she picked up on her shorts could be matched to the recovered mower later on, if necessary.

"See, no – whoops!" Timothy tripped over a rake and went down on his knees in between Katy's legs, grabbing onto the bronze flesh of the girl's thighs for support.

Katy reflexively tightened her legs around the man's skinny neck to hold him upright, her teenaged body, and pussy, flushing with the hot, sweaty feel of Timothy's big hands on her bare legs. She swallowed hard, staring down at the trapped man. "You will tell me who cut your lawn then, won't you, Mr Gruder?" she said, not resisting the impulse to squeeze a little harder. A good detective has to use any advantage presented to her.

Timothy's glasses steamed up, as he moved his head forward in the heated vice of the girl's thighs in an attempt to get some air into his windpipe. Until his thin lips inadvertently bumped into the crotch of Katy's shorts, kissing up against the thin, damp material.

"Mmmm!" Katy murmured, tingling all over; but especially where the kneeling man's lips met her private lips. She eased the pressure on his neck, as he increased the pressure on her crotch.

He kissed up and down the front of Katy's fresh-smelling shorts, hands rubbing, caressing her firm, sun-burnished thighs. And then he licked – dragging his long tongue over the teenager's clothed pussy.

"Ooooh, Mr Gruder!" Katy moaned, the man's heavy, wet tongue feeling so very good on her buzzing slit. She closed her eyes and leaned back, digging her sparkly fingernails into the wooden edge of the workbench.

Timothy gripped the girl's thighs and ardently stroked

her thinly veiled pussy with his tongue, long, soothing, sensual strokes that left both of them gasping. Then he swirled the hardened tip of his tongue all around the exact spot where her clit lay hidden and swollen beneath her pink cotton shorts.

And when he lightly nipped her there, Katy impetuously bumped his reddened face back with her flushed mound and popped her shorts open. She scooched them down and off her legs, so that the mature man could kiss and lick and suck her bare pussy.

He gulped. "Groovy, I see someone likes to keep their own lawn nice and trimmed," staring at Katy's bald pussy mere inches away. Its puffy, pink folds glistened wet and inviting. Like the overheated teenager herself.

"Eat me, Mr Gruder!" she yelped, clutching his ponytailed hair and jerking his head forward. "Please, eat me!"

His open mouth slammed into her naked pussy, and he tasted sugar and spice and everything naughty, before eagerly lapping at her slit, chewing on her petals, and sucking up her tangy wet excitement.

Katy tore a hand off the man's bobbing head and stuck it up her tee, grabbing onto a shimmering boob and squeezing, anxiously pinching and rolling the stiffened tip, as Timothy clung to her bucking thighs and licked and licked her pussy. He began fingering her juicy flaps apart and capturing her button between his lips, and then sucking. Sending the teen dream into sweet spasms of joy, and squeals of delight, her smooth-muscled thighs almost crushing his head again.

He barely had time to lick her hot, sticky juices off his lips, when she pulled him up and she went down herself – on him. Fumbling the zipper of his bell-bottoms open and pulling his long, hard cock out of his tie-dyed shorts.

"Righteous!" he groaned, the kneeling girl gripped his dong at the furry base and enveloped the cap with her lips. The shock of her warm, wet mouth engulfing his hood had him shaking all over.

Katy earnestly stared up at the towering man and pushed her head forward, swallowing up more and more of his pulsating pipe, until Timothy's meaty cockhead bumped the back of her throat and she gagged slightly. He instantly grasped her dangling pigtails and pumped his hips, fucking her mouth; faster and faster, his pistoning cock deliciously cushioned by the teen's wet, beaded tongue, sealed tight between her soft, full lips.

Katy blinked tears out of her watering blue eyes and desperately sucked air in through her flared nostrils, the man's churning meat filling her mouth and jamming her throat. And then really, truly filling and flooding her mouth, Timothy yanking on her pigtails and bucking and bawling, "I'm trippin'! I'm trippin'!" Hot, salty spunk spurted into Katy's mouth and down her gulping throat.

She eventually swallowed his story, as well, after he gave her the name of the landscaping company he'd used to cut his lawn: Greenleaves Inc. They'd paid a visit to his property especially early just that morning.

Katy pedalled over to the Selkirk County Library and googled everything she could find on Greenleaves Inc. Then she perused the local newspaper microfiche files to find out even more about the company, and its reclusive owner, Leif Bjarnson. Not all detective work was as exciting as what had gone down in Mr Gruder's tool-shed, the teenager well knew.

She plotted Leif's home address into her GPS device, and let it guide her to his house three miles over. Peddling hard, her brown legs pumping and red pigtails flying, perspiration shone on her cutely resolute face.

She found the man's place – a large home with an assortment of expensive cars out front. A pretty fancy set-up for a guy who filed a pretty modest tax return (Katy had computer hacking skills she only used in case of an emergency, like now).

After snapping a few pics of the property with her digital camera, she rode over to the Greenleaves Inc. compound a little further down Highway 1. Just in time to recognise the small, dark, shifty-looking character getting out of a battered Ford pick-up and entering a corrugated-metal building. He looked just like his picture in the paper.

Katy trailed after him.

"Hello, 'Greenfinger'," she said, catching the man by surprise in his small, cluttered office behind the counter out front.

He spun around and glared. Then smirked, when he saw it was only an eighteen-year-old girl. Though a very pretty redheaded one at that. A 'Red Roses' pin-up calendar hung from the wall in back of his crummy desk, July's beauty: a scantily-clad Rita Hayworth, in living colour.

"Where'd you get that name from?" Leif Bjarnson asked, his voice high-pitched and jittery.

Katy gripped the straps of her backpack and glanced around the rat's nest of an office, noting the forty-five year-old's weakness for redheads. The chest area of her stretched-out tee and the crotch area of her bunched-up shorts were damp with moisture, but her voice was calm, as she said, "Oh, I've done my research – Greenfinger. Did a bit of jail time for counterfeiting way back when, didn't you?"

He snarled, "What'd you want, cherry pop?"

Katy twisted a copper-coloured pigtail around her finger, watching the man intently watch what she was doing to her hair. "My dad's mower was stolen. I was, um, just wondering if you'd seen any 'hot rides' show up here recently?"

Leif licked his lips, staring at the girl's tightly-braided flaming tresses, her tight, sun-bronzed body blazing out of her skimpy shorts and tee. "Me?" he squeaked. "Naw, I ain't seen nothin' like that. I run a clean operation. Check in the back, if you don't believe me."

The amateur girl sleuth took the nervous man up on his offer, and they walked further into the rusty building. Back into a cramped repair/storage area that contained seven broken-down hand mowers and nine limp-stringed weedwackers. Plus one very new John Deere X740 riding mower, with the plates missing.

Leif climbed onto the yellow seat of the high-end grass-cutter and gripped the leather-wrapped steering wheel and casually claimed, "I just bought this baby last week – beauty, huh?"

"Uh-huh," Katy agreed, admiring the expensive machine's fine lines. Then impulsively shucking her backpack and leaping onto the mower herself, right into Leif's lap. "It's a real beauty, all right," she breathed into the man's startled face.

The landscaper flushed with the heat from the teenager's bare legs straddling his legs, her heaving, handful titties so close. He inhaled the sweet, tangy scent of her eager, young, curvy body, his mind clouding and cock hardening.

Then he tore his dazed eyes off her prominently poking nipples and looked at her hanging, red pigtails. And that did it. He grabbed onto the twin copper, coiled love handles, pulled Katy's face close, and kissed her.

She jumped in his lap. Before promptly returning the man's fierce kiss, wrapping her arms around him and pressing her body into his.

"Fuck, yeah!" Leif grunted.

"Yes! Oh, yes!" Katy gushed.

Leif's slick tongue slithered through the girl's plush lips and bumped into her tongue. Their slippery tongues entwined over and over, feverishly. The both of them surged with shimmering heat, locked together atop the shiny new riding mower.

Leif rained kisses down on Katy's freckled face, and fine hair. Katy closed her eyes and sighed, wriggling with pleasure in the man's lap. Diving one of her hot little hands down in between his legs, she grabbed onto the large appendage that had swollen up there, and excitedly started rubbing.

Leif pulled Katy's top out of her shorts and, peeling it up her quivering bod, popped it off. Baring the teen's dewy brown boobs, her wicked-hard, inch-long nipples burnished an even darker brown by a season of surreptitious sunbathing at the abandoned rock quarry. The hard-breathing man stared at the girl's treasure chest, then clutched her boobs, squeezing the firm, warm, young flesh in his sweaty hands.

"Yes, Greenfinger!" Katy squealed, shuddering with delight.

She grabbed onto the guy's short, slightly greasy hair, as he attacked her trembling boobs with his hands – really mauling them – and then with his mouth, devouring them. He spun his snake's tongue around first one jutting pink nipple and then the other. Before sucking the entire spongy mass of a tit into his mouth and tugging on it.

Katy went wild, tearing the man's shirt open and

192

going after his hairy chest, grasping and squeezing, licking and sucking on his hard, red nipples. He dug his dirty fingers into her shining hair and jerked when she ran her tongue up to his neck and her hand down into his dungarees, grabbing onto his pulsing cock and tugging.

Leif hastily unbuttoned and unzipped, and Katy yanked his cock out of his pants and out into the open. She enthusiastically pulled on its ribbed, throbbing length with both of her hands, as the two of them urgently kissed and frenched.

The precocious teenager stood up on the tractor and shoved her shorts down, exposing her bald, brimming pussy. Then plopped back down into the mature man's lap and tilted her legs up so that he could pull the itty-bitty garment right off.

She grasped his pulsating cock and rose up and then down on it, guiding the rigid member in between her dripping lips and deep inside her sopping pussy. All the way in, until her bum touched down on his thighs.

"Fuckin' A!" Leif growled, buried to the balls in the redheaded teen's tight, oven-hot pussy.

"Fuck my cunny, Mr Bjarnson!" Katy shrieked into Leif's face, wrapping her legs and body around the stunned man. Overcome with frenzied girlish passion, her lover's cock filled her to bursting with bliss.

Leif pumped his hips as best he could, as Katy bounced up and down in his lap, in rhythm to his fuck-thrusts. They desperately clung to one another, his straining dong churning her love tunnel, almost splitting her in half. Their impassioned gasps and groans, the hot, wet smack of his thighs against her rippling bum, echoing erotically in the steamy, sex-funked repair and storage space.

Until Katy suddenly wailed with all her heart, "Oh

my God, Mr Bjarnson! I think I'm gonna … come!" She surged with sweet, soul-drenching joy, her pigtails flying and boobs bounding. The man's upright stake stoked her full of fiery adult delight.

"Fuckin' A, Red!" Leif hollered, thrusting with abandon, wide-eyed watching the teenager flower and erupt with total release. He grabbed onto her jumping boobs and just about squeezed the buzzing tops off, furiously plugging her pussy, the girl's hot juices soaking his cock and lap.

And then he exploded, spouting blazing ecstasy into the screaming, quivering teen, sperm blasting out of his pumping, pussy-sucked cock, orgasm scorching him right down to the sexual core.

He was still dizzy and disoriented, when Katy suddenly leapt up off his drained cock and spun around, landing back down in his lap with a bare-bummed splat. Then she cranked the key on the riding mower and shifted into gear and drove the machine right through the hidden door between two piles of spare parts.

They burst into the mower chop-shop in back doing twenty miles per hour, Katy whipping up her arms, and boobs, and whooping with triumph. Her dad's brand-new Toro Classic GT/315-8 sat there shining under a single hanging lightbulb, still mainly in one piece.

"See, I measured the length of the building before I went in," Katy informed the smiling Sheriff. "Then paced off the distance inside when I was talking to Mr Bjarnson. And there was a twelve-foot discrepancy – where the chop-shop was hidden. Which I suspected all along, given Greenfinger's dirty dealings in the past." She blushed when she said 'dirty dealings'.

Sheriff Perkins handed the beaming teen sleuth her

Honorary Deputy Certificate, as the gathered crowd cheered and cameras clicked. Then the bald, beefy law enforcer leaned in closer to the dolled-up girl, squeezing her hand and suggesting, "Maybe you'd like to ride along with the night-shift sometime, huh, sweetheart?"

Katy grinned and bobbed her red head, her bright blue eyes twinkling. "I might just investigate your offer, Sheriff," she cooed. "Crime-solving is sooo satisfying, after all. And nothing beats real hands-on training!"

Nightcap
by Elizabeth Cage

Common sense should have told Robyn that February in
Dresden would be cold. Bitter cold. After all, it was still
winter back in the UK. She hadn't quite expected what
seemed like arctic conditions. She had packed skirts,
tights, woolly socks and jumpers and worn them all – at
the same time. The evenings were worst of all. Walking
down the romantically lamplit streets, she pulled her pink
beanie hat over her ears and pushed her gloved hands into
her jacket pockets, but her fingertips still felt numb.

Still, there were two things to be grateful for. Firstly,
the Marketing Conference was over. She loved her job but
three whole days with fellow IT sales reps was enough for
anyone. So now she had some time to sightsee before her
flight home the following afternoon. Which brought her
to the second thing she was glad of. Dresden was a truly
beautiful city. When the taxi had collected her from the
airport, she had been awestruck by how romantic and
magical it looked, the golden glow of the streetlights
reflecting on the river as they crossed over the bridge. The
old buildings, steeped in history, were strikingly elegant
and she felt like she was stepping back in time as they
pulled up outside the 4-star hotel opposite an expensive-
looking shopping mall. She was only steps away from the
famous Frauenkirche Church and the River Elbe. Far too
romantic to be here alone, she reflected, her breath rising

in spirals in the chill night air. Walking through the quiet streets, she contrasted a Saturday night in her home town, dodging drunken lads and noisy ladettes, and stepping over vomit and discarded chip wrappers, with this civilised place where the only people she encountered on the street were just leaving the local theatre or opera house, smartly dressed and properly behaved. It was like a different world.

Even so, Robyn couldn't remember ever feeling this cold. It seemed to penetrate her very bones. She needed heat – and quickly. There were plenty of welcoming restaurants and bars down the main street and she stepped inside the nearest one. The warmth hit her in the face as soon as she opened the door but it was unbelievably welcome. Then she noticed how crowded the bar was and realised there was nowhere free to sit. Reluctantly, Robyn turned to go when a smiling waitress appeared and gestured her up some stairs to another level where a small alcove overlooked the rest of the bar. It was perfect. Tucked away, yet still in company, there being two other small tables, both occupied by couples.

Unlike some of her female friends, Robyn never felt self-conscious about eating or drinking alone in public. The whole Bridget Jones singleton thing hadn't done women any favours, she reflected. One couple was young, probably in their twenties, clearly besotted with each other, their fingers entwined as they gazed continuously into each other's eyes. She smiled. Twenty years ago that could have been her. The other couple was late middle-aged and long-term married, she decided. They were not as tactile but shared the comfortable familiarity that comes with mutual longevity. She wondered where she would be in twenty years time – ten even. She couldn't think further ahead than a month at the most, sometimes only a week and that was how she liked it. Minimal planning – offering the opportunity for spontaneity. Robyn enjoyed not knowing what was around the corner. That's what made life fun.

She sipped deliciously hot, strong coffee with plenty of brown sugar. By the time she'd finished, the young couple had left and their table was quickly filled, this time by a dark-haired guy wearing trendy, steel-rimmed glasses. Robyn had always had a thing for men in glasses. They changed a person's appearance, so when the glasses were removed, it was like someone different. Like having two men for the price of one, she reflected. A vulnerable Clark Kent and a masterful Superman. She tingled as she imagined it.

Robyn was amused, if somewhat surprised, when he ordered a beer for himself and water for his clearly devoted companion sitting on the chair opposite. The man was attractive, probably in his thirties, with clear, chalk-blue eyes and sharply defined features. But it was his gorgeous companion that really got her attention. Robyn couldn't help staring. It was all she could do to contain her desire to touch …

Finally, in her faltering German, she went over to the table and said, 'Excuse me, but may I?'

The man smiled and nodded as Robyn reached out and stroked the adorable dachshund that looked up at her with liquid brown eyes.

'I love dogs,' she explained.

'So I see,' he replied adding, 'English?'

Robyn laughed. 'Is my accent that bad?'

'Not at all, your German is good,' he replied in impeccable English. 'She is called Freya by the way. And she loves fuss and attention.'

'Hey, don't we all,' said Robyn fondling the dog's

silky ears, adding, 'I'm Robyn.'

'Karl Herzliebe.'

'Herzliebe. Doesn't that mean love heart?'

'Literally, it is heart love.'

'What a romantic name,' said Robyn.

He shrugged, blushing, and, embarrassed to have made him feel awkward she said, 'Well, I'm named after a garden bird.'

'Renowned for its red …er …plumage,' he replied, glancing at the tight figure-hugging crimson sweater that showed off her ample cleavage to maximum effect. Now it was her turn to blush. She stepped back towards her table, deciding she should leave him in peace, but he said quickly, 'Don't go. Freya likes you. See?'

The dachshund was wagging her tail, eager for more attention.

'You are very welcome to join us.'

Robyn hesitated but he had already got up and pulled a chair out for her.

'Thank you.' She sat down and their legs touched. She noticed he did not move away. Neither did she.

'This wouldn't happen in the UK,' she said.

He looked puzzled. 'So, English men do not flirt with women in bars?'

She shook her head, laughing. 'I meant Freya. Dogs wouldn't be allowed in bars or restaurants like this, not unless they were guide dogs. They certainly wouldn't be sitting on a chair at the table like a person.'

'Why not?'

'Health and safety, I suppose, or food hygiene laws.'

'Does it offend you?'

'Not at all. I think it's really nice. Like I said, I'm very fond of dogs.'

'Do you have a pet?'

'Not allowed. I rent a top-floor flat and no dogs or cats are permitted. But I do voluntary dog walking for a local animal charity, most Sundays.'

'That's kind.'

'I enjoy it and it's good exercise, while performing a service.'

He eyed her mischievously and for a moment she wondered if he was going to make a smutty remark. He didn't say it but she guessed from his expression he was probably thinking it.

'Can I buy you another drink?'

'I'll have a cappuccino, thanks.'

By the time the drinks arrived, Freya had jumped up onto her lap and was lying on her back, demanding a tummy tickle. Robyn obliged.

'I'm afraid she will moult all over your lovely sweater,' he apologised, his eyes lingering.

Robyn shrugged. 'That doesn't worry me.'

She felt perfectly relaxed. It was an unexpected pleasure, enjoying a drink with a sexy stranger and his cuddly pet, in a nice warm bar in a romantic city.

As steamy froth dribbled down the over-full china cup, Robyn licked it up, catching the milky fluid before it escaped. Karl Herzliebe reached out and wiped it from her mouth with his long fingers, letting them linger. She flicked her tongue over her lips, catching his fingertips.

She decided to pick up on his earlier remark. 'Are you flirting with me?'

'Would you like me to?'

Robyn smiled sweetly, enjoying the game. 'Delicious coffee. Hot and satisfying. Just what I need.'

When it was time to leave, he said, 'Let me walk you back to your hotel.'

'Thanks but it's only round the corner from here. I

don't want you and Freya to go out of your way.'

'It's not. I live close by. Very close. Here actually.'

'Here?'

'I own the bar.'

'You own it?'

He nodded.

'It's a very nice bar.'

'My flat upstairs is even nicer.'

'Really?'

'Like to see it?'

'Maybe.'

'I can offer you a nightcap.'

'You trying to tempt me?'

'Maybe.'

'What kind of nightcap?'

'One you'll never forget.'

Robyn didn't need asking twice. Minutes later, she found herself pinned against the wall of a black and chrome designer kitchen in an upmarket penthouse, her tongue down Karl Herzliebe's throat as he pushed his hand up her heavy skirt and rolled down her woolly tights. Robyn loved the contrast – from civilised conversation in a bar to frantic, hungry sex in a matter of seconds. She fumbled for his shirt buttons, almost ripping the fabric in her haste, needing to feel flesh. She wanted to eat him.

He ran his hands over her bare legs and curvaceous hips, groaning with delight as they tongue wrestled and Robyn clawed at his back. They were both impatient. Quickly, he hooked his fingers inside the flimsy fabric of her lacy boyshorts, probing and stroking, exploring her wetness, while his other hand tried to lift her tight-fitting red sweater. Robyn helped him haul it over her head, and he moaned appreciatively when it revealed her voluptuous breasts, trapped in a black push-up bra. Though not for much longer. He reached for the hook fastening at the back and muttered, 'Your bad boys are free now,' as her breasts sprang out.

Side-stepping the pile of clothes on the floor, Robyn pushed her large breasts forcefully against his bare chest as she unfastened the leather belt of his jeans. When she yanked the zip down, it was his turn to spring out.

'I think your bad boy is free too,' she grinned, grasping the hard rod with both hands and plunging her mouth over the purple head, gorging herself. She felt his fingers burying themselves in her hair as he cradled her head, pulling her closer while she sucked and licked. His cries grew louder and louder until he said. 'Stop. I want to taste you first.'

Robyn obeyed and released him from her mouth, allowing herself to be lowered onto the polished wood floor so that Karl Herzliebe could bury his head between her wide open legs. His appetite matched her own and as he licked and nibbled enthusiastically, she thought he would suck her dry. She was in heaven.

After a while he lifted his head to remove his glasses, saying, 'They are all steamed up. And sticky.'

Robyn shook her head. 'No. Leave them on. For now.'

He seemed surprised, but said, 'OK, kinky bitch,' before diving once more into the depths of her soaking pussy. She was unable to hold back any longer and her passion and greed soon overwhelmed her. As she came loudly, her body wracked by waves of intense pleasure, he crouched over her and rammed his glistening cock into her open mouth, muffling her cries. His groans soon overtook hers in volume as he quickly exploded, and Robyn's mouth was filled with hot, sticky fluid, which trickled down her chin and spilled over onto her breasts.

They lay side by side for a while, panting hard, getting their breath back. Eventually, Robyn sat up and said, 'I'm surprised you can see anything through those glasses. What a mess. I think they need cleaning.' She leaned over him, her still-hard nipples brushing against his face. 'So you can take them off now.'

She had experienced the wild side of Clark Kent and loved every minute. But now she wanted Superman.

'You look different without your glasses,' she said, putting them out of harm's way on the glass coffee-table.

'Better?'

'Different. Just as sexy. But different.'

And she kissed him gently on the forehead. 'So I get another man for Round Two.'

He laughed. 'You are a very greedy, kinky bitch. But I did promise you a nightcap you would never forget. Stay there.'

He rolled over onto his side and got to his feet, leaving Robyn basking in her afterglow. When he returned, he was holding two tumblers of whisky.

'Cheers,' he said, offering her the drink. It was good whisky, strong yet smooth. Robyn always found the smell of whisky a turn-on. Her German lover took a mouthful, carefully parted her legs and lowered his head once more. Robyn sighed, anticipating more tongue action, and gasped in surprise when she felt a hot, almost stinging, sensation as he released the whisky he'd held in his mouth into her swollen cunt. Her eyes widened as he followed this with the tip of his tongue, giving her an exquisite massage, the sensations heightened by the alcohol.

'Delicious,' she murmured appreciatively, closing her eyes to savour it.

When he'd finished, and she was close to the edge

once more, he sipped more whisky, took the glass from her trembling hand and kissed her, letting her inhale the mixture of her own juices and the golden liquid. She felt intoxicated and her head was pounding. Gently, he pushed her back onto the floor and straddled her, his stiffening cock already sheathed in rubber. He slid easily into her gaping opening, and this time, having dealt with their previous urgent hunger, he took things slowly.

Robyn tried to hold back as long as she could, loving the intensity of sensation experienced during the moments before climaxing, but she soon gave in, allowing her body to drown in ecstatic waves. Karl Heart Love flipped her on to her side and spooned her while gently fucking, his arms wrapped around, his hands caressing her large nipples, groaning softly as he came.

'Satisfied?' he whispered.

Robyn smiled as she nestled against his warm, naked body. 'Mmm. For now. Although another whisky nightcap might be in order.'

'There's something I have to tell you,' he said. 'I have another pair of glasses. Would you like me to put them on – for Round 3?'

Robyn grinned. 'Yes, please.'

'I thought so.' He squeezed her nipples. 'Kinky, greedy bitch.'